your b&b or mine?

a Maple Cove novel

MELISSA WEST

Entangled Publishing, LLC
2614 South Timberline Road
Suite 109
Fort Collins, CO 80525
Visit our website at www.entangledpublishing.com.

Bliss is an imprint of Entangled Publishing, LLC. For more information on our titles, visit http://www.entangledpublishing.com/category/bliss

Edited by Alycia Tornetta
Cover design by Heather Howland
Cover art from Shutterstock

Manufactured in the United States of America

First Edition November 2015

Bliss
an Entangled imprint

For my sweet Rylie

Chapter One

"Where you want me to drop you, Ms. Hale?"

Savannah focused straight ahead, ignoring the sad look from her cab driver. She had never planned to unload her situation on him, but then he asked her where she was heading and she said Maple Cove and suddenly there were no words, only tears. It took exactly ninety minutes to drive from Atlanta's Hartsfield-Jackson airport to her small town in Georgia, and she had spent eighty-five of them spilling her guts. A part of her felt shame for showing her emotions so fully—the driver must have thought she was insane—but then, it wasn't every day that she lost her mama.

Savannah's eyes filled with fresh tears, and she blinked them away. She had spent the last five minutes touching up her makeup, sure that if she walked back into Maple Cove looking like a mess of a woman, she would only convince her town that she did nothing else but cry. She could almost hear the McLain sisters now. *Leave crying and return crying, that's our Savannah Hale.*

Sighing, she pointed to the four-way stop just ahead. "You can let me out there. Mayor Young prefers to keep cars off Main Street."

"Ms. Hale, I don't feel right leaving you to walk down the street with all your bags. Can't I just drive you to the bed-and-breakfast?"

Savannah stared down Main Street, a memory hitting her of her father beside her, standing in that very spot, a wide smile on his face. He had said that arriving at Maple Cove's most successful bed-and-breakfast was an experience, and it wasn't a full one unless you walked down Main Street to get there. Her mother agreed, but said patrons would want to park at the B and B, so as a compromise they had two parking lots—one on site, and one at the end of Main Street. Of course, during prime season, they enlisted the service of a horse and carriage company for older guests—or those wanting a leisurely ride.

"Thanks, but I think I'll walk," Savannah said, her heart heavy. It was hard losing her daddy five years ago to a heart attack, but it was nothing like this. Losing her mama made her feel like a little girl again—a lost little girl, with no one around to hold her hand and guide her through her life. She hadn't even gotten married yet, or had kids. Who would adjust her veil at her wedding? Who would she call in the middle of the night when her newborn baby refused to stop crying? The pain felt like it would break her in two.

"Ms. Hale?"

Savannah shook herself from her thoughts. "Oh, I'm sorry, Martin." She forced herself to smile at the old cab driver, wishing he were a local. She could use someone around Maple who didn't speak in Southern sugar slap—a sweet smile on their face while they insulted you.

Martin stepped out of the cab and grabbed Savannah's carry-on suitcase and laptop bag from the trunk. "Are you sure I can't walk you in?"

Savannah laughed. "Trust me, that would only make it worse." She could only imagine what the town would say if she had someone carry her bags for her. They would accuse her of forgetting where she was from. Of being uppity. A *Yankee*. And while she knew she would eventually have to defend herself and her decisions to the people she'd once called friends, she wasn't prepared to do it today.

She grabbed the handle to her carry-on, slung her laptop case across her shoulder, and set off down Main Street, her spine pencil straight.

From this vantage point, the town looked so innocent, like something out of a Norman Rockwell painting—all cute awnings and wooden benches and rocking chairs. Dogs asleep outside their owners' stores. Wrought-iron lampposts that were as custom to the town as its people.

The memory hit so suddenly she didn't have time to brace herself, to shield her heart—swinging around a lamppost, laughing with her head flung back, her stomach full of butterflies for the boy beside her. It had been her and Will's first date, and even then, she knew she'd love him forever. Sadness crept through her heart at the memory, followed immediately by guilt. Forever wasn't a reality. Not for Savannah.

And not that she deserved it.

She had made it a third of the way down Main Street, to the official start of the shops, when the smell of Maple's

Bakery hit her nose. Her stomach grumbled as she imagined the morning buns and apple turnovers and blueberry muffins, all still warm from the oven. She had been so desperate to make it home after receiving the call about her mama that she took the first flight out of Boston, ignoring her body's pleas for her to grab a cup of coffee — or six. She had been hopeful when she landed, but the line at Starbucks had been too long for her to wait.

Now, she contemplated what she would rather do — face the gossip brigade head on in order to grab a coffee and one of those Oh-my-God-this-should-be-illegal blueberry muffins, or starve in hopes that no one would see her.

She had just resigned herself to starve when, like an alarm had sounded announcing her arrival, familiar faces appeared one by one in the shop windows and then stepped outside their doors for a better look.

Pastor Parkins waved a cheerful hello, and then immediately went over to sit with the McLain twins outside Annie's floral shop. His head drew close to theirs, no doubt discussing all the rumors about Savannah. She tried to ignore their looks, the obvious distaste the McLain twins had for her now. No one left Maple Cove and returned without feeling the weight of the sisters' stares, their judgment. She wanted to shout that she knew their stories, too. Like when the twins switched places with their husbands for a week and the husbands were none the wiser. Or when Anna Beth got caught stealing a petit four from the bakery. Savannah knew their stories. *All* the stories. The difference was, they didn't seem to care who knew what about them.

Savannah cared. Her great-great grandfather was one of the founders of the town, and with that legacy came a wealth of expectations for how a Hale should behave. And Savannah had met those expectations all her life, except for one tiny infraction. One slip. Something no one truly knew, but most speculated about all the same. And maybe she should regret it. Maybe she should drop on her knees and ask God to forgive her. But the truth was she didn't regret it. She only regretted what happened after.

Oh well, at least now she could get coffee.

Pushing through the door of Maple's Bakery, she released a slow moan at the aromas. *Cinnamon and spice and everything nice*, her mama used to say. She bit her lip and tried to remind herself that crying wouldn't bring her back. Nothing would.

Inside, the bakery was painted canary yellow with pictures of desserts framed on the walls. Scattered here and there were mosaic-top bistro tables, each a different color — red, blue, green, orange, and on and on. To the right was the glass display case, showing everything Martha had made that day, and while there were always certain favorites, she liked to throw in a few surprises to keep her fans on their toes.

Savannah glanced quickly around the small bakery, hoping to avoid eye contact with any of the townspeople seated at the tables. She had naively prayed the bakery would be slower at this hour, but judging by the line at the register, it was still the only place in town you could get a fresh pastry and a decent cup of coffee.

Taking her place in the back of the line, she kept her head down in hopes that no one would approach her, but then a squeal came from her left. *Oh no.* She spun around in time to see arms thrown out and a black-haired person yanking her into a hug.

Savannah pulled away to find her baby sister standing before her, only her sister no longer looked at all like a baby. Or like a strawberry blonde.

"Oh my God, Leigh," Savannah said, reaching for her sister and pulling her into another hug. "You...you don't even look like yourself. You're so..."

"Grown up?" Leigh added with a small smile.

Leigh Hale was the youngest of the three Hale kids, and to Savannah she would always be sixteen and boy crazy. She had been an artist from the moment her chubby toddler fingers could hold a crayon, and to this day had spent every dollar she had trying to make a living at it.

Now she ran the local art museum, offering up unique exhibits and generally fixing her name in the Will-Never-Fit-In Maple Cove Hall of Fame. Her hair, which had once been the same strawberry blond color as Savannah's, was now as black as a summer storm, and her clear blue eyes were lined in thick purple liner. Savannah wondered how she could handle wearing so much makeup, especially now, when tears could fall any moment.

But then, maybe their mama's death hadn't impacted Leigh the way it had Savannah. After all, Leigh had been there with her. She was able to tell her she loved her and kiss her cheek. She'd had her day in and day out, unlike Savannah, who had left for Boston eight years ago and only returned once, when her father had died.

How had both her parents left this world before sixty-five? It was unfair to lose them so early, when many people lived into their eighties these days. She deserved to have those twenty years with them, needed those years, but her mama had been so crushed after her father's death, they all suspected she would die of a broken heart. Maybe that was why cancer sought her out—it knew she longed to be reunited with Daddy.

Whatever the reason or fairness, her parents were gone.

Savannah gripped her chest, wondering if she would ever feel normal again or if she would always be a breath away from tears. Sighing, she focused back on her sister. "Is Jack here yet?" she asked as she reached the front of the line and placed her order.

"No," Leigh said, "But I wanted to warn you about—"

Before she could finish, another squeal sounded from their left and Savannah remembered why she had packed her bottle of Advil. Everyone in Maple Cove spoke in one of two tones—excited squealing or angry screaming. This time the squealing came from the closest bistro table and the pack of platinum blondes circling its tiled top. Savannah glanced at each of them, lost to their names, and then recognition hit her. They were her old friends—Brenna, Hannah, and Dana—but they didn't look like she remembered. They used to laugh at how similar their names all sounded, but now the similarity did nothing more than add to Savannah's headache. Where was her coffee?

Forcing a smile, she tried to recall if the three women had always been quite *this* blond or if that was a new development—along with the size of their breasts.

"Hi," she said, faking excitement, but then their expressions all changed to pity and she cringed as one by one they came over to hug her and offer their condolences.

"I'm so sorry about your mama," Hannah said. "We always loved her."

"We did," the others chimed in, which caused Leigh to roll her eyes. Leigh was never one for faux kindness and tended to judge anyone that smiled for too long.

Savannah nudged her with her elbow before she said anything overly Leigh-like and then motioned to the register, where the bakery owner, Vicky, stood grinning, fresh pastries and coffee in hand. "Well, it was good seeing you," Savannah said to the women.

"You, too!" They started back for their seats, when Brenna added, "First Logan, now Savannah. Who are we going to see next?"

Savannah skidded to a halt, nearly dropping her coffee. "Wait, what? Who did you say?"

Brenna smiled knowingly. "Logan Park. You remember him, don't you?" Her expression and the rise in her voice made Savannah's cheeks flame. She thought of the time she and Logan went to a movie together after he'd returned home from deployment, only to find Brenna there with her boyfriend of the week, beaming with delight at Savannah's apparent naughtiness. Because Logan wasn't just any guy. He was Will's best friend since third grade, which meant Savannah couldn't look at him without causing a few eyebrows to lift.

He and Will had been inseparable the moment they met. Where one went, the other followed. So it shouldn't have been a surprise that they entered the army together. Only it was a surprise—a devastating one.

Savannah still remembered the look on Will's face when he'd told her he had enlisted, how excited he had been while she fought back tears.

Half the town thought he'd propose before he left for

Afghanistan, and a part of her worried he might. But then she looked into his eyes his last day in Maple Cove, kissed his cheek, and sensed the hesitation there. The same hesitation she felt. Because while she adored and respected Will, she refused to marry a man unless she was 100 percent his. Mind, body, heart, and soul.

And the problem was, another boy had confused Savannah's heart that year. A boy she thought had always hated her. A boy she forced herself to put out of her mind long before she and Will were ever a thing.

A boy named Logan Park.

Still, Savannah had loved Will, had belonged with Will. So they spent a year more apart than together, Will away in Afghanistan and Savannah in Maple, playing the part of his loyal girlfriend, just waiting for him to return home so they could fall in love with each other all over again.

But that wasn't her story.

Instead, Logan showed up at the old swing at Cross Creek Plantation that fateful Sunday…without Will. Suddenly Savannah stopped caring what everyone thought and focused on her own survival. And God did she ever need Logan. He stepped in, catching her before she could fall, supporting her through the tears, the anger, the depression that refused to lift. He understood her pain because he felt it, too.

So when Logan asked her to go see the latest summer Marvel blockbuster, she went. She needed to feel normal again, she needed to lose herself in another world—she needed to feel the warmth of a boy beside her, one whom she had always cared for, nothing around them but darkness and silence. One outing became two, then once a week, then all the time.

And then everything changed.

Now, her eyes shifted away from the three blondes, unable to hold contact. "Sure. I remember him."

Brenna's smile stretched, and Savannah knew exactly what she was thinking without her having to say a word. The rumor. It started just after Logan left for his second deployment, and while no one had the guts to ask Savannah directly, they had all made up their own accounts of what had happened that day. As it was, no one knew the truth. No one except Savannah…and Logan.

The thought of him being back, somewhere in town, possibly walking Main Street right this second, sent her mind racing and her heart into a frenzy. What did he look like now? What did he do for a living? Where had he ended up? And maybe the one question that plagued her the most—when he lay in bed at night, his day done, did he feel his life was complete or did he have regrets? Surely he had regrets…at least one.

Savannah had no idea, but as her thoughts switched to memories, she found herself growing more and more angry. Who was Logan to come back here? And why now? Well, she'd just avoid him. That's what she would do—avoid him and pretend that none of it mattered. Because it didn't matter. Not then and certainly not now.

Blinking hard, Savannah held her head a touch higher, ignoring her former friends' gossipy stares. She wouldn't fall prey to those looks, not again. She wasn't some nineteen-year-old girl anymore. She was twenty-six, an adult.

So why did she feel so small?

Despite her success in Boston, and her ability to move

up the ranks of the consulting firm where she worked, she still wanted to please the people of Maple. The desire to have them like and respect her ran deep.

Leigh looped her arm through Savannah's and pulled her close. "Well, we have things to do. You know, *real* things," she said with a condescending smirk. "You should try it." And then she grabbed the handle of Savannah's suitcase and directed her back out the bakery door and down the sidewalk, past the McLain twins and Pastor Parkins, who were still gossiping, to the familiar cobblestone road at the end of Main Street, which curved and bent its way back to Maple Cove Bed and Breakfast, the Hale family business and their childhood home.

They stared up the oak and dogwood tree-lined drive to the two-story blue Victorian home, its wide front porch empty except for the six rocking chairs that had always sat there, and the white porch swing where Savannah's mama used to read to the kids before bed during the summer.

"Have you been there since…you know…she left?" Savannah asked, her heart so heavy she wanted to wrap her arms around herself to keep it from falling to her feet.

Leigh reached for Savannah's now empty coffee cup and passed her the handle to her suitcase. "I didn't want to go in alone. You and Jack weren't here, and I just…couldn't. I couldn't go in."

Savannah draped an arm around her sister, who immediately became uncomfortable and shrugged out of it. Leigh was never one for affection and had always hated showing her emotions. Clearly, some things never changed.

"I need to grab some paperwork from the museum," Leigh said, refusing to meet Savannah's gaze. "Okay if I see you later?"

Savannah nodded. "Yeah, yeah. Of course," she said.

They said their good-byes with the promise that Leigh would join Savannah at the bed-and-breakfast once their brother Jack arrived that afternoon.

As soon as Savannah crossed onto the road and out of sight of the town gossipers, she reached up and wiped away the beads of sweat that had dripped down her neck. She'd forgotten how suffocating spring could be in Maple, how it hit a person like a blanket of heat. It felt more like summer, as though Mother Nature just shrugged and went on to the scorching season, bypassing the lighter months.

Savannah had just decided to pick up her suitcase, which refused to roll easily across the cobblestone, when a tingly feeling rippled down her spine, settling at the base of her back. Her skin pricked with awareness and familiarity and something else—something she'd tucked away long ago. Before she could lift her eyes to confirm what her body already knew, a deep voice breathed, "Savannah?"

Her gaze drifted up, and her mouth fell open. Well, at least now she had the answer to the question of what he looked like. Because standing on the front steps of the bed-and-breakfast, wearing business slacks and a white collared shirt and looking like he stepped out of a magazine, was the one person who could make this day worse.

Logan Park.

The only person in the world who knew the real reason Savannah left Maple.

Logan stared down at Savannah, at a loss for how a girl as pretty as she had been could become even more beautiful as a woman. Her once slim frame had filled out in all the right places—from the tank top that stretched across her full breasts to the khaki linen pants that hung low on her hips and clung to her ass. She was all woman now, and the temptation to pick up where they had left off ate away in his mind. Only, nothing had changed, and he still didn't deserve her. Which was why he'd spent the better part of his twenties trying to forget her. The problem was…there was no forgetting a girl like Savannah.

To this day, he still remembered the first time he met her. Billy Walsh had just called Logan's mother a whore, and though Logan wasn't really sure if she was—at nine he had no idea what that word meant—he didn't like Billy's tone, and so it made sense to drive his fist into Billy's face. The whole class surrounded them on the playground, and then when Logan won, they were all, *Poor Billy*. Everyone except Savannah. She walked over and lifted Logan's chin, studying his already swollen left eye and *tsking* loudly as she glared back over at Billy. "That wasn't nice of him," she had said. Then she helped him inside and cleaned his bloody lip and right there, at that moment, a tiny piece of his locked heart opened up. But he soon realized Savannah Hale wasn't his kind of girl.

She was Will's kind of girl.

Logan pushed his thoughts away and started down the steps of the bed-and-breakfast. "Can I help you with your bags?"

She tightened her hold on the handle of her carry-on "What are you doing here?" she spit out.

Well, that was fast. He had hoped to get in a few niceties first, but Savannah was never one to bullshit with him. Everyone else? Yeah. But once her walls came down after Will died, they'd never gone back up around him. Her shoulders would relax, her eyes soften, like for once she could breathe.

"I'm sorry to hear about your mother. She was an amazing lady."

Savannah crossed her arms and tilted her head, her expression as plain as day. She didn't want his condolences, or anything else from him. Logan almost laughed at her tenacity. Even after suffering the loss of her mother, she wasn't a broken woman. She could take care of herself, which was one of the things that drove him so crazy about Will—he'd treated her like a delicate flower, when Savannah was less a flower and more a tall oak, whose limbs refused to break even in the worst weather.

"You didn't answer my question," she said. "What are you doing here? What do you want?"

Logan smirked. "Well, now. That's two questions."

Savannah's face lit with anger, and again Logan had to force himself not to laugh. She was different now, yet the same, that angry sass all too familiar.

During the Homecoming parade senior year, Logan had convinced Will to help him decapitate the mascot. He had never seen Savannah so mad. But then again, he had gotten used to her scolding when he was a teenager. Back then, Logan was all about pranks and baseball and girls, and Savannah was as studious as they came. He had always known her wings would carry her somewhere. He just never imagined they would carry her as far as Boston.

"I want to know, right now, what you're doing on my

property, Logan Park."

Biting back a smile at her use of his full name, his gaze lifted to Savannah's face, and suddenly his bullshitting and smirk disappeared. At first glance, she appeared as strong as ever. But within her eyes, there lay a sadness that cut straight through his chest, settling in his heart. He didn't want to have this conversation. Not yet. She had just lost her mother and needed time to grieve and heal, and he knew she would grow hostile as soon as he said the words. Plus, he was enjoying the brief hints of easiness they shared. Well, maybe not easiness, but she wasn't yelling. Again, not yet.

"I'm in town on business," Logan said, glancing left to the outdoor garden. In its center, a couple sat on a stone bench, the man reading to the woman, the look on her face so full of love that Logan wondered if the expression was fake. Surely that sort of love didn't really exist. At least not in his world.

"I didn't ask what you were doing in town. I asked what you were doing *here*."

Their eyes locked, and Logan thought he saw a touch of hope in her eyes, like maybe she wanted to see him after all. He took a step toward her, unable to remain still with her so close after so long. A rush of adrenaline shot through him, memories weaving through his mind. Soft touches. Warm smiles. A thousand conversations about nothing that meant everything.

But then the look disappeared from her face, and he swallowed hard, knowing there was no way around it—he had to tell her. He opened his mouth and calmly said, "I'm with Hartridge and Long. Their Atlanta office."

She stared at him, her face a mix of confusion and

annoyance. "And you are telling me this why?"

He cleared his throat. Surely she had received the paperwork by now, but by the expression on her face, she knew nothing of his company, which meant she had no idea. Closing his eyes, he took a step back. "Look, we'll talk later. After you've settled everything. I'm sure you—"

"Logan Park, you leave without explaining, and I will roll my carry-on over your toes. What does Hartridge and Long have to do with you being at the bed-and-breakfast?"

With one more long sigh, Logan forced himself to look up. He was a lot of things, but he wasn't a coward. Stubborn? To the bone. Selfish? He had his moments. But he wasn't a coward.

"Hartridge and Long is a real estate investment company."

"So?"

He drew a breath and released it, forcing the words out. "The real estate investment company slated to buy the bed-and-breakfast."

Chapter Two

"Get off my front steps!" Savannah shouted, anger taking over all reasonable thought and action. She'd had enough. She wanted to step inside her childhood home and allow the warmth of her parents' memories to wash over her. She wanted to cry in her old bedroom and beg God to bring her mama back.

What she didn't want to do was stay there in front of Logan Park, the one person who could break her, when it took every bit of her strength to stand. She couldn't handle it. And now he was there to buy *her* bed-and-breakfast? No, no, no, no, no!

"Anna, look, it's—"

"Don't you dare call me that. We aren't friends. We were *never* friends." Savannah knew her words were harsh, even untruthful, but what was she supposed to say? He'd left, and now he stood on the steps of her bed-and-breakfast, talking about buying it, as though it weren't the most hurtful thing he could possibly say to her. The weight of everything pressed down on her shoulders, her chest. Any second she would crumple.

She drew a rattled breath and tried to focus on Logan without seeing all the things in him she'd once adored. The way his long lashes shadowed his eyes. The way his hair always had a just-woke-up look about it. How could a person change so much and yet remain exactly the same? "Please, leave. I need to sort out my mama's burial, and I can't do that with your face looking over my shoulder."

Logan's careful facade cracked, and the smirk dropped to a frown. "Again, I'm so sorry for your loss. But when you're settled, we need to talk about this. We're willing to offer you a very generous amount of money."

Savannah covered her eyes with her hands, wishing she could block out everything. The pain. The memories. God, the memories... "Just leave already."

Logan walked down the steps and around her, sending a chill up her spine as his lemongrass scent hit her. He still smelled exactly the same—all earth and freshly laundered clothes and a yearning for something important but he hadn't quite figured out what. Her heartbeat kicked up at the thought, and she pushed it aside. The man before her wasn't that Logan, though she wasn't sure if she'd ever truly known him at all.

She started up the steps, when Logan called out her name. She dropped her arms to her side in defeat. "What now? Are you here to steal the dog, too?" She motioned to the collie curled up on the front porch.

Logan stuck his hands in his pockets and looked at the ground before tilting his head up and peering over at her. It was the same look he used to give her that summer, when no one else was around, like he could see through her soul with just the slightest glance. "I'm sorry about Jane. I am. But we *were* friends, Savannah. We were a hell of a lot more than friends." And then he continued down the winding road and out of sight before she could respond.

With a shudder, she tucked away the emotions she felt at his words, the doubt and insecurity she'd harbored for all of her adulthood, and pushed her way through the screen door and into the foyer of her family's bed-and-breakfast.

The smell of old wood and apple cider and a thousand precious moments hit her, stopping her in her tracks. Dust floated in the air, refusing to settle, like even it had no idea what to do now that Jane Hale was gone. Savannah's mama had an air to her, an ability to make people see things her way. To make them feel special, loved. She was the reason the business had been so successful, even garnering articles in *Southern Living* and *RedBook*. Twice. The Maple Cove B&B had built a reputation across the South as the place to go for comfort and friendship. And now it was over.

A shudder worked its way down Savannah's back and before she could help herself she was sobbing. Why hadn't she come home more? Why hadn't she called her mama more? Why, why, why? She kneeled on the floor and cried into her hands, ignoring everything around her, wishing she could sink into the floor and hide until the funeral was over. It wasn't until she heard a man clear his throat that it occurred to her that she might not be alone.

Panic gripped Savannah's chest. She hadn't asked Leigh if the bed-and-breakfast had guests. She just assumed they would close it down for business until everything could be settled, but clearly...

Savannah peeled open one of her eyes and turned her head to the left, to the small dining room full of tables, where guests ate their meals. Sure enough, fate loved her today, and the room overflowed with people, all of them staring at her with a mix of expressions on their faces.

"Is this going to be a regular occurrence?" the old man closest to Savannah asked. "Because if so, I think I'd like a discount on my rate."

Savannah scrambled to her feet, her cheeks on fire as she wiped away her tears with the heel of her hand. "No— it— No it's not, sir. It—" She glanced around the room for help, and her gaze locked on the white-haired Mrs. Cooke, who had helped Savannah's mama run the bed-and-breakfast since Savannah was in diapers. Her heart leaped at the sight of her, tears threatening their return. "Mrs. Cooke?" She was as close to Savannah's mama as they came.

Walking over to the open doorway, Mrs. Cooke smiled sweetly at the guests and said, "Enjoy your breakfast. The biscuits are rolled fresh every morning." And then she closed the French doors and drew their blinds, set down her teapot on the water tray in the foyer, and wrapped her wrinkled arms around Savannah. "Dear God. I never thought I'd see you again, Savannah Jane."

Savannah's bottom lip trembled at her full name, and she buried her head into Mrs. Cooke's shoulder. "I'm sorry. I had no idea we had guests."

"It's all fine, honeybunch. They've seen worse. Now let's get you fixed up before your brother and sister arrive. They need your strength, even if you don't feel it yourself."

Savannah nodded. Her strength. She thought of Logan

out on her front porch, and how her heart had slammed to a halt the moment she saw him. How could she feel such relief and at the same time such anger at the sight of a person? It had taken all her effort not to rush into his arms and settle into his chest like she had after Will's funeral. But that Logan Park wasn't the same Logan Park who broke her heart, who made her question if their friendship had all been in her head. So, unsure how to handle him earlier, she'd gone with yelling. Because at least if she yelled, she wouldn't cry.

So much for strength.

Logan settled into a chair in the back of Southern Sandwich and Fudge, ignoring the stares that seemed to follow him since his arrival in Maple Cove. The smell of fresh pancakes and syrup, mixed with the sizzle of frying hash browns, attacked his senses in the best possible way. He drew a breath and let it wash over him. If only his father didn't live in town, Logan might have liked to move back to Maple, but living in the same town as Canton Park sounded as appealing as having his fingernails ripped off. His upbringing had been enough to make him want to avoid the man for the rest of his life.

Unlike Will, who'd had a perfect childhood and supportive parents, the definition of Southern breeding, Logan's father drank liquor like most people breathed air. His father had wanted him to work down at the cotton mill a town over when he graduated, and when Logan told him he wanted to go to college instead, his father laughed. "What would a loser like you do in college?"

Logan's mom was no better, spending more time in bed with either men half her age or men who had no business talking to anyone other than their wives. Alcoholic for a father and a whore for a mother—how could Logan amount to anything? He couldn't and wouldn't.

Except for Will.

Will pushed him to care about school, to join the baseball team, and get his head out of his ass. And everything was great, until Will started talking about Savannah. The very girl who had stolen a piece of Logan's heart all those years ago. But as she started coming around more and more, it became apparent that Logan was a shadow—a black shadow that did nothing more than ruin their happy lovers glow. And he resented her for it. Resented that she'd chosen Will over him. Didn't she feel their connection? He guessed not, until that one day at the lake.

She had gone out by herself on her family's old bass boat, only to have the battery die on her. As it was, he figured she would rather swim home than take a lift from him. Their relationship had become a mix of sarcasm and avoidance. But he had been working as a guide that summer, and there was no one else around. Just him in a guide boat, and then it was the two of them, talking as he secured her boat to his and took her to her father's truck parked at the dock.

She begged him not to tell Will—saying that she was embarrassed, that he would judge her for going out on her own and he would be right. Logan hadn't noticed until then that Savannah fidgeted whenever she thought she had lost control of the situation. And that day, Savannah was fidgeting like a crazy person. Unable to deny her, he agreed and they spent the next hour getting a new battery from her dad's truck, then switching it for the bad one in her boat. And damn if by the end of that hour it wasn't done—her name carved into his heart like reckless footprints in cement.

He ignored his feelings for years out of respect for Will, but once he realized how deep they ran, he had no idea what to do. For a while he refused to talk to her, refused to even look at her, which did nothing more than cause one of the biggest arguments he had ever had with Will. He'd told Logan he was an asshole, and all Logan could think was, "You have no idea how right you are."

They left for basic training a few short days later, and in what felt like overnight, they were deployed for ten months to the Korengal Valley in Afghanistan. And for the first time in Logan's life, he understood fear. How it clung to a person, attached to each breath, refusing to lift. The "Valley of Death," it had been called, and the name proved right. It took five men in his unit...including his best friend.

Everyone knew Logan should've been the one to die, but God never worked by the opinions of man. Certainly not Logan's. So he'd drawn up his courage and found Savannah out on Cross Creek Plantation, legs swinging as she sat in the old, handmade wooden swing that hung from the giant oak, a small smile on her face until she lifted her gaze to his. Before he'd even said a word. her eyes turned shiny and her hands began to shake. They clung to each other for hours after he told her, the start of a friendship between them. He'd told himself she needed him, but really, he'd needed her...

Now, he leaned back in his chair at Southern Sandwich and ran his encounter with Savannah over again and again in his head. It hadn't gone at all like he imagined. Sure, her running into his arms, smiling and planting her deliciously full lips on his was a little dramatic, but he hadn't expected her to be quite so…enraged.

The waitress appeared at his table, a coffeepot in hand. "Whatcha having, honey?" she asked, her hip cocked against the table. Logan tried to place where he knew her and failed. Someone from high school, he felt sure. But then, Logan was never one to remember people from high school. He looked at her a little too long, and her bubbly demeanor quickly turned to disdain. "Sara Beth Trent. We dated."

Logan cringed. Ah, he remembered now, though *dated* seemed a little strong of a word. If he remembered correctly, they went on one date when he returned from his third deployment — a short stint in Kuwait — and ended up in the back of his Jeep. Man, he loved that Jeep. He had never owned a luckier truck.

"Right. Of course," Logan said, wishing he had tried a little harder to lie, but lying never came easily to him. An uncomfortable silence settled between them, so he spouted out his order. "I'll have scrambled eggs and grits. Bacon on the side." Sara Beth *tsked*, but filled the empty coffee cup on his table and strutted off, shaking her head.

He was going to have to be more careful now that he was back in town. He tried to remember how many women in Maple he had been with, but couldn't come up with real faces or names. Too many, clearly. All in an effort to forget the one who fled to Boston and who apparently hated him now. Not that he could blame her. After all, he was the one who convinced Will to enlist. It was his fault Will was dead. And then Logan had done the unthinkable, and everything went to shit.

The bell on the shop's door dinged, and in walked Jack

Hale, Savannah's brother. Jack was something of a celebrity in Maple Cove, after entering the minors and quickly being called up to the Cardinals. He had a five-year stretch where he was the best shortstop in baseball, but something changed after their father died, and while Jack was still good, he wasn't the player he once was. Like the passion in him had disappeared.

A crowd formed around Jack, asking for autographs they already had. After signing a few, Jack peered around the shop and his eyes stopped on Logan, a smile breaking across his face. He nodded to him and then started his way. Years ago, they had played on the same team in high school, and though they had never stayed in touch, they were still friendly. Well, more so than he and Savannah. Though that might not be saying much.

Jack motioned to the chair across from Logan. "Care if I join you?"

"Nah, sit." Logan kicked the chair out, and Jack sat just as Sara Beth came over, her fiery gaze now on Jack. Logan guessed he wasn't the only one to mess around with Sara Beth. Unperturbed, Jack placed his order and then settled back in his chair.

"How are you holding up?"

Jack shrugged as he poured a cup of coffee. "Could be worse, but could be a hell of a lot better, too."

"You seen your sister yet?" Logan asked, hoping maybe Savannah was angry at the world and not just him. Death could do that to a person. He knew that first hand.

"Not yet. Leigh has me picking up some lightbulbs at Jim's, then I'm heading over. Hey, you wouldn't be free after this, would you? I have to move a bookcase and could use an extra set of hands."

Logan grinned as Sara Beth set his breakfast in front of him. "Nope. Not busy at all."

"But how are we supposed to get up there?" Savannah scratched her head and stared up at the attic door in the ceiling, where supposedly her mama had kept the paperwork about the bed-and-breakfast in a safe. Their family attorney had her will, but nothing about how to actually run a bed-and-breakfast, or about the financials, which after Logan Park's claim, she might not want to see.

She thought of Logan the way she'd last seen him before today, all broken and wrecked with grief, and of then the man on her front steps earlier, not a care in the world. How could he even come to her with talk of selling the bed-and-breakfast when her mother had just died? What kind of person did that? A heartless person, that's who, and Savannah had known for eight years now that Logan was the definition of heartless.

Focusing back on the task in front of her, she jumped into the air to try to reach the tiny cord hanging from the attic door, but at five four—on a good day, when she stood really, really straight—her fingertips only grazed the end. "Ugh!" Hands on her hips, glaring at the attic door like it had single-handedly created all of her problems, she wondered why her mama opted to put the safe in the attic anyway. Why not the study? Or with their accountant? Or any one of a thousand other places? But then her mama had been known to do a lot of things that made little sense to Savannah.

"What now?"

Mrs. Cooke shook her head. "I don't know, child. I think there's a ladder in the basement. Want me to go hunt for it?"

Savannah waved her on. "No. I'll go. But can you check the dining room and make sure no one's waiting for anything?" She eyed her watch. How had four hours passed? She felt like she had just arrived, and already it was lunchtime. One thing she knew about the guests of Maple Cove's Bed and Breakfast, they expected breakfast by eight and lunch by noon, every day. She didn't want to disappoint them.

"Of course. You'll call me if you need anything?"

Savannah smiled. "Oh, rest assured, I won't call. I'll scream."

Mrs. Cooke's eyes twinkled. "I've missed you around here. Won't you stay?"

Savannah opened her mouth, but no words came out. She couldn't stay. Her life was in Boston now. She had finally gotten promoted to account manager at Zelner Consulting and was handling her own accounts. She loved her job, even if the hours were excruciating and the pay, for the amount of hours she worked, left a lot to be desired.

But instead of saying any of that, she said, "I've missed you, too," and hugged the woman close, because she *had* missed her. She had missed all of them.

Mrs. Cooke went on down the creaking hardwood steps and around the swirling white banister at the bottom and then out of sight. Savannah released a breath. She didn't want to scare the employees. Not yet. Rumors of the bed-and-breakfast being on the market had already made their way around town, and she could see the question in each of their faces when she met them. They wanted to know if she would take over for her mother. She wished Leigh or Jack could do it, but that wasn't possible. Leigh was too flighty and Jack was still contracted with the Cardinals, which left only Savannah.

Sighing heavily, she made her way down the steps to the door under the stairs, which opened to another set of steps leading to the basement. Savannah remembered being petrified of the basement as a kid. It was dark and damp and generally looked like the kind of place devil-worshipers would go to sacrifice small animals. Now she opened the door and started down the rickety steps, reminding herself that she was an adult. There was no reason to be afraid of the dark. Right? Though as the chilly air hit her, and goose bumps rose across her skin, she wasn't convinced.

Once at the bottom, she reached up and pulled the chain on the light. A tiny stream of light spread out across the open area and she started forward, ignoring the goose bumps that refused to settle. Shivering from the cold, she wrinkled her nose at the musty smell and the spider webs hung like Halloween decor from wall to wall.

She glanced around for the ladder, prepared to dash in, grab it, and dash out. Finally, she spied it against the back wall and cursed her forever-bad luck. "Fantastic. Thank you. Couldn't you hang out over here?" she said then shook her head at herself, because now she was talking to a freaking ladder.

Knowing it wouldn't magically land in her hands, she drew up her courage and dashed across the basement, grabbed the ladder, and dragged it back to the steps, her heart hammering and her hands shaking more than they should. Laughing at her silly fear, she lifted the ladder with the intent of carrying it upstairs, but the top rung immediately hit the low ceiling of the steps. She eyed the stairs and then the ladder, and was trying to figure out how she could get it upstairs without accidentally knocking a hole in a wall when the distinct sound of running water hit her ears. She leaned the ladder against the wall and crept forward, listening. Where was that coming from?

Pushing aside spider webs, she edged to the farthest corner of the open room and pressed her ear to the door there, listening. That was when she caught sight of the water trickling out from under the door. Oh no. *Oh no, oh no, oh no!*

She opened the door and gasped. Inside, an exposed pipe sprayed water like a yard sprinkler on a hot summer day. Everything in its path was drenched—boxes, blankets, an old couch—everything.

Savannah rushed into the room and tried to wrap her hands around the pipe, but that pressure must have been the final straw. The pipe burst, shooting water out in all directions and soaking Savannah from head-to-toe. She screamed out for help, while trying frantically to stop the rush of water.

"Savannah! Are you down here?"

"Yes! Help!" Before Savannah had time to process who she had just called for, Logan was in the doorway, a smirk on his face.

"Need some help?"

Clearly, this day was trying to break her.

Logan's grin widened as he took in Savannah's appearance. She was soaked through, like she had jumped into the

Cherokee without a thought of a swimsuit. He opened his mouth to jokingly ask if she needed a towel, when his gaze landed on her white tank top and the lacey bra that barely covered her perfect, round breasts. He cleared his throat and forced himself to focus on something other than how her nipples stood at full attention. Likely she wouldn't appreciate him calling out just how exposed she was at the moment.

"Where's the water main?" he shouted over the pounding water.

"What?" Savannah tossed up her hands like she wanted to scream—or cry. "I don't know! What's a water main?"

Logan bit back a smile and edged into the room, looking around until he found where he could turn off the water. Once it stopped, Logan pushed his soaked blond locks out of his eyes and peered over at Savannah. "You all right?"

She shook her head, and Logan thought she might break down. Instead, she burst out laughing, the sound so amazing it was as though it were meant just for him. "If Mama could see me now," she said, still laughing. "She always said bad luck followed me around like a shadow. I guess she was right."

"Ah, now, I don't call it bad luck. I call it interesting," Logan said as he rolled up the sleeves of his shirt and shook out his wet hair. He glanced up to find Savannah watching him, the anger he felt from her earlier replaced with something else. He swallowed hard and took a step toward her, his mouth open to say the words he had wanted to say all day—that he was sorry, that he was wrong to leave, that he missed her—when Jack and Leigh came running into the room.

"Oh, shit!" Jack said, examining the inches of water.

"What did you do?" Savannah's eyes lit with rage and she darted for him, her fists clenched, but Logan stepped between them. He knew all too well how feisty Savannah could be, and he would hate to see Jack return to Saint Louis with a shiner.

"It's just an old pipe," Logan said. "I'll call Jim. He'll get this fixed up in no time."

Savannah glanced at Logan. "Thank you." Her expression was careful, her voice low, almost a whisper, and he wondered if it was because she didn't want to thank him or if it was because she remembered how they had been before.

"You're welcome." Their eyes connected again. A single beat, a moment, but Logan couldn't deny the electricity that moved between them. He spent eight years trying to get over the woman, and then in just a few hours, he was back to that day in the rain, just the two of them under the weeping willow by the lake at Cross Creek Plantation, his heart hers for the taking.

He nodded toward the doorway. "I'll go check in with Jim."

"All right," Savannah said, her cheeks suddenly flushed. She bit her bottom lip and Logan's gaze dropped, everything in him wishing it were his teeth taking that bite instead of hers.

He cleared his throat and met her gaze once more, shocked to find her watching him as intently. Was it Logan's imagination, or was she just as affected by him as he was by her?

Chapter Three

Savannah sat down on the front steps between her brother and sister, all their gazes focused on the apple tree straight ahead. The three of them had often climbed it when they were younger, plucking fruit and hiding from Mama.

How was it possible the tree had survived but their mother hadn't?

The thought caused a fresh wave of emotion to bubble up inside Savannah, and she cleared her throat in hopes of pushing it back down.

"So what now?" Leigh asked.

Just then the screen door behind them opened then banged back into place. Fix one: the water pipe. Fix two: the screen door.

From the door came a middle aged couple, the woman all pearls and curly-haired head shaking, the man following quickly behind her.

"I'm sorry, is there a problem?" Savannah asked.

The woman stopped in front of her, hand on her hip, lips pursed. "Yes, I'd say there is. The water doesn't work in our room. Or any other room. We're leaving. And if you so much as consider charging our card, you'll hear from our attorney."

Savannah's eyes widened. "What? The water's off? It can't be. It's—"

Then Logan came through the same door, his shirt now rolled to his elbows and pulled loose over his slacks. "The water's off until Jim can replace the pipe. It should have been done a long time ago."

Irritation—and, okay, a little bit of desire, but she was ignoring that particular reaction—raced through her. "What are you still doing here?"

Logan started to answer, when she tossed up a hand. "No, hold that thought. One disaster at a time." She returned her attention to the couple now walking away from her, their bags in tow.

"Wait, I'm sure the pipe will be repaired any minute and everything will be fine. Please come back." But they were already around back of the bed-and-breakfast now, likely getting into their car. "Oh my God, I've been here all of twenty minutes and already we've lost a patron."

Leigh walked up to her. "Not *a* guest. I think we're losing *all* our guests." She pointed to the screen door, and sure enough, a line had formed by the front desk, irate expressions on most of the faces.

Savannah started inside, her voice more shrill than she liked as she tried to answer the surge of complaints that hit her the moment she crossed the threshold. "Okay, how about free dinner to everyone who stays. We'll have the water fixed and—"

"Not today. Maybe tomorrow at best. Jim's not sure he has the right part."

Savannah whirled around, unable to hold her anger in another second. This was just like that time when she got stranded in her daddy's boat, Logan voicing his opinion like he was Jesus Christ himself, that hint of condescension behind his deep, Southern drawl. "This. Is. All. Your. Fault," she said, poking him in the chest with each word, hoping her finger could somehow cause permanent damage, or at least a really painful bruise. But instead, a spark jolted from her finger up her arm, reminding her of the first time he took her hand, traced the lines on her palm, and told her everything would be okay. And she believed him. God, did she ever believe him.

Shaking the memory from her mind, she took a step back, desperate for some space so the feeling would dissipate and she could go back to raging.

"My fault?" Logan shook his head. "You know, you haven't changed at all. You're still crazy as hell!"

And just like that, the rage returned. "*Me*?"

"Yes, you. I came here to help, I set everything up with Jim, and somehow I'm the one to blame? Oh no, can't be Ms. Perfect Savannah Hale's fault." He turned away from her and went outside, huffing as he walked down the drive. "Just like that day on the lake," he called back.

She gasped and followed after him. "What did you say?"

"He said, 'just like that day on the lake,'" Jack answered from the front porch.

"I heard what he said, Jack," Savannah hissed. "I was asking what he meant."

Logan spun around. "I saved your ass from being stranded in the middle of the Cherokee, and you blamed Jack for not returning the spare battery on the boat, and then me for putting a scratch on the piece of crap as I pulled you to the dock."

"Hey! I didn't steal the battery," Jack called defensively.

The right side of Savannah's head throbbed, the first of what she knew would be many migraines. Funny how she suffered from them all her childhood, yet she didn't have a single headache from the time she left until today. The day she returned home. The day she was reunited with the likes of Logan Park.

"First, I didn't blame you for the scratch," she said to Logan, then her eyes cut to her brother as she pointed her finger. "And yes you did. You put it in that bass boat you bought off Miles Blake."

Jack's face relaxed, the memory coming back to him. "Oh, yeah. Man, that was a good boat. What happened to that boat?"

Deep breath. Deep, long breath.

"You sold it to Will," Logan answered, his voice lower now.

"Ah."

Savannah's gaze landed on Logan, her heart suddenly heavy with the weight of death. And then it was as though she were back there—Logan coming to tell her Will was gone. She remembered his slow walk to her, his refusal to lift his head, like he no longer knew how to stand straight. Knew how to see clearly. Knew how to be.

How to exist.

The weather had been entirely too perfect, not a cloud

in the sky, the sun so bright she had to squint as she looked up at him. Then he dropped onto his knees in front of her and shook his head slowly, and they'd both just crumbled. Never in her life did she think she would lean on Logan Park, but that day she collapsed against his shoulder like he was her last hope for life.

They cried for what felt like forever. He eventually pulled her into his lap, and they just sat that way, on the ground, crying and talking. Still to this day, the words they said made no sense at all. And finally, when their bodies could cry no more, they lay back in the grass, hands linked for fear they would lose themselves again if they let go, and Logan told her about the first time Will saw her.

It was as though Will himself was there telling the story, and she wondered how Logan remembered it so clearly. At some point day turned into night, but neither moved. They just continued to talk until, like their tears, their words ran dry. And then there was only sleep, out under the sky, no blanket for warmth. What could it do to warm them anyway?

Now, Logan asked, "What can I do, Anna?" And for the first time since she returned, she felt like there was someone in Maple who cared about her and her needs.

"Jim—"

"I took care of it."

"You paid him?"

"I took care of it."

Savannah didn't know what to make of Logan helping her after she had been so hateful, but how else could she act after what he did? She was afraid if she relaxed she would tell him all the things she longed to say so many years ago, and she couldn't go there. Anger felt easier.

"I need to sort out everything for the receiving and burial."

Jack and Leigh took turns looking at each other, and Savannah contemplated turning her anger on them instead of Logan. At least he was helping.

"We need cleaning stuff," Savannah said.

"I can get that," Leigh replied a little too quickly. Since when was she willing to go to the hardware store without an argument?

"I'll help her," Jack chimed in, pushing off the steps like he had just received a Get Out of Jail Free card.

"It doesn't take two to get stuff to clean up, you loser," Leigh said, which immediately caused a sharp retort from Jack, and then they were arguing over who knew what about cleaning, and finally Savannah's migraine decided to spike, her eyes burning at the edges, her neck aching as pain radiated from the crown of her head to her back.

"Just get out of here already, before I throw you both out."

Her siblings stopped to look at her.

"You know, you were a lot nicer before you moved to Boston. What, do they add lemon to the water to make you extra sour or something? You should—"

"All right," Logan said, cutting in, his voice filling Savannah with relief, which irritated her all the more. His voice shouldn't make her feel better. "Everybody take a breather. Y'all get to town. Savannah, go in, figure out what you need for the receiving and burial."

A part of Savannah wanted to argue with him, though she had no idea why. She wanted to argue for the sake of arguing with anybody or anything that might argue back.

Especially Logan Park. Maybe if she screamed enough she wouldn't feel so empty inside.

Leigh and Jack walked down the main road, still bickering, and Savannah turned her attention on Logan. She swallowed hard. "Thank you."

"You're not alone here."

"Yeah? So why does it feel like I am? I've never felt more alone in my life."

"You just lost your mother. It's hard to exist when the person who taught you how no longer does."

"Do you think it ever feels better?"

Logan considered her, and she expected him to say time heals all, or some other nonsense that everyone says but no one believes. Instead he said, "No. But I think it might get easier to carry." He backed up and turned for the road. "See you later, Savannah Hale."

The morning sun had long since disappeared behind the trees, the faint smell of honeysuckle lingered in the air, and with all the guests gone now and without the worry of new ones to come, Savannah walked to the wooden sign her daddy had made by hand and flipped it over. The word CLOSED read so very final that she barely made it inside, the screen door flapping shut behind her, before the tears returned.

Unsure what else to do, she walked upstairs and disappeared into her old room, not wanting to go over the details of burying her mama when she felt so weak. For now, she wanted to feel her mama's life, not work out the details of her death.

As she stepped into her former room, the smells of home came wafting back to her. Old candles still sat on the shelf beside her bed, half burned, half covered in dust. It surprised her that her mother hadn't changed it into another available room at the bed-and-breakfast. But then Savannah knew her mother had hoped from the moment she'd left that she would return. The thought made her heart ache in a way she had never experienced, and needing to fill it with something, she walked over to her closet and opened the door, flicking on the light to find the space still full of old Christmas Barbie dolls in their original boxes, Precious Moments figurines, and two boxes of keepsakes that simply read "My Savannah."

Rising onto her toes, she pushed aside the box of CDs from her high school days and grabbed the shoebox she'd tucked away there before she left. A part of her had wanted to bring it with her, fearful her mother would find it and toss it without realizing what lay inside. But leaving with memories was tough enough. She couldn't imagine bringing with her things that could stir it all back up again.

The old wrought iron bed rattled as she sat down on the edge of it, placing the box beside her, not yet committing. But then she looked out the half circle window to her left and saw a full moon rising in the sky. There was nothing but time now—Leigh and Jack would likely eat dinner out. With reluctance, she kicked off her flip-flops and scooted back on the bed, crossing her legs crisscross applesauce, the box in front of her.

"It's just a box, Anna," Savannah told herself, using the nickname her daddy had used every time he spoke to her. A name Logan picked up somewhere along the way.

She tried to remember the first time she heard him use it, if it was a joke or serious, but she couldn't remember. The only thing she knew was that he never used it around

Will. Like he needed something that was just between them. Maybe he— No. Logan spent more time avoiding her than talking to her back then, so what would she know about his feelings? Besides, she refused to allow herself to go down that road again.

Reaching for her cell, she started her favorite playlist— the one she played whenever she wanted to feel, not think, and then gently placed the box top beside her on the bed. Her eyes immediately went to the first photo inside.

They were all there—Jack, Leigh, and Savannah, their parents standing like posts on the outside of them, Cape San Blas's white beach stretching out behind them. They had rented a house for a week every summer for all of her childhood, and that summer was no different. Their smiling faces were brown and red from too much sun, and Jack had rabbit ears up behind Leigh's head, but there were nothing but positive memories from the day. Her gaze landed on her mama, and she had to swallow hard to keep from sobbing.

Jane Hale always wore a patient, easy smile, and her eyes twinkled with knowledge she would never share. Savannah often wondered what her mother had experienced before meeting and marrying Savannah's daddy, but Jane would only say her life began when she married Andrew Hale, not a day before it.

Her hair was styled in the same shoulder-length waves she wore until she died, though in the photo her hair was the same strawberry blond as Savannah's, not the snowy white it became as she aged.

The headache began to ease as Savannah let her emotions out, no longer holding in her tears for fear someone would come by and she would need to get back to running things.

The next photo was of them all at Jack's major league debut. Their father hated flying, but he took the trip eagerly to see Jack play. That was the proudest moment of Andrew Hale's life, and he would recount Jack's homerun at his first ever major league game to anyone who would listen.

Savannah continued through the stack as if moving through time. First the childhood favorites, then the few accomplishments they had experienced—Jack's debut, her and Leigh's college graduation—and then she reached the point where her daddy was no longer in the photos. The family reunion. Christmas. Savannah felt her heart growing heavy again. They would now have photos without either of their parents, and how could you call it a family get-together without the two most important members present?

Finally, she reached a light blue piece of construction paper, and for a moment her hand hovered over it, unsure if she wanted to continue. She knew what lay behind it would only make it harder for her to breathe, and already her nose was stuffy from crying, her throat thick from the effort to stop. But there were times when the sadness felt so tangible she wanted to add to its weight, push the pain as far as it would go. Maybe to drown it out, or maybe to let it consume her. Whatever it was—a cure or a drug—she knew she needed to continue.

Lifting the paper, she laid it on top of the family photos, her eyes on the mirror above her desk, directly across from her. Tiny keepsakes and notes were tucked into its frame. The sight of her red, splotchy face was so foreign that a part of her wanted to stop the madness now, but she couldn't. So she let her eyes drop slowly back to the box, immediately landing on Will's senior photo.

With a shaky hand, she lifted the photo out of the box, her other hand going to her mouth. His dark hair curled out at the edges, refusing to be contained, messy yet somehow perfect. His honest blue eyes stared into the camera, his smile wide. Will never wanted anything but the happiness of others. There were times when Savannah listened with skepticism as people talked about the dead as though they were heroes, but with Will it was true.

A rumble sounded off from her stomach, reminding her that she hadn't eaten anything since the muffin that morning. Wind rattled the window outside, and Savannah thought her brother and sister would likely return within the hour, without any food for her if she didn't request it soon.

She picked up her phone and dialed Leigh's cell.

"Hey."

Loud music and loud talking met Savannah's ears. "Where are you?"

"What did you say?"

"I said, where are you?" she said louder then jerked her head toward the door, fearful she had disturbed guests until she remembered there weren't any.

"At Sal's, eating with Jim, Logan, and Jack."

"Wait—you're with Logan?"

"What?"

Sighing heavily, Savannah said, "I'll text you."

"Fine, bye."

She immediately texted her sister to bring home a cheeseburger and fries and a Coke, because grief allowed you to eat whatever you wanted without guilt. Then she set her phone beside her again, eyeing it to see what Leigh would say back. A part of her wanted Logan to ask about her, and for Leigh to text her on his behalf, but that was stupid and besides…

Her gaze fell on Will's photo and she sighed again. "I know."

She turned the photo over and placed it neatly in the stack with the others, then went for the next, a smile forming on her face. Will stood beside a cherry-red Corvette. It was old and nothing especially beautiful to look at, but he and Logan had rebuilt the engine themselves, slowly bringing the car back to life. When they finished, they all went for a ride, only to end up out of gas on the side of the road, the boys arguing over whose fault it was. All Savannah could do was laugh.

Still smiling, she ran her finger over the photo, her nail catching on the right edge, where it had been folded down the center, Will on one side…Logan the other. A memory came back, of sitting in the same spot on her bed, tears on her cheeks as she folded the photo in half. It was the day she came home from the lake incident, when Logan had towed her back to the dock, making a promise between them that he wouldn't tell anyone.

Somehow something had changed after that, when she'd looked into his eyes at her father's truck. She no longer saw the reckless kid she had always known, but a boy who was less boy and more man, with a kindness in him that maybe had always been there but she never quite noticed.

The moment had stretched between them, and then he'd cleared his throat and she'd looked away, but it was done— the start of something she could never finish, though every time she saw him she ached to see if that kindness in his eyes would return once more.

Having only the one photo of Logan, she would reach for it, telling herself she wanted to see if the kindness showed, but really she just wanted to look at him without anyone around to judge her. The fold should have worked, kept her focus where it needed to be — on Will. But it didn't.

She would see Will on the other side of the Corvette, smiling into the camera. Smiling at her. Savannah would toss the photo back into the box, angry and guilt-ridden all over again. She'd eventually forced herself to stop looking at it, locking it, and all the emotions it conjured, away.

Until the day Will and Logan left for basic training. She'd taken the photo out once more, giving herself permission to look at him. After all, she had no idea if she would see him again.

Now, with no one around to watch but the shadow of guilt that always followed her around, she flipped the photo to the other side, allowing the tingly sensation she felt every time she saw Logan to spread from her chest to her head, making her almost dizzy. Warmth followed in its wake as she stared down at the boy she once knew, and wondered if he was the same man who stood on her front porch earlier today.

Who was Logan Park now? And was he as dangerous to her heart now as he had been then?

Chapter Four

Logan drove back to Atlanta first thing the next morning, needing to wrap up a few things and grab some paperwork. And, okay, so he could get away from Savannah and think. Interstate 75 was as congested as ever, and he wondered why he didn't leave at five like he wanted. Then he remembered the late night with Jack and Leigh.

The whole reason he'd joined them was the hope that Savannah would show, so he could explain that he wasn't in town to hurt her. Buying the B and B wasn't to hurt her. None of it was to hurt her—it was all for Will. His double majors, his career choice, his travel, his every accomplishment and success were all for Will. But she'd never showed, and even if she had, how could he explain? He couldn't. These experiences weren't his to share; they were Will's.

So, after a few too many beers and no Savannah, he walked out of Sal's to the small motel just down the street. He should have known she wouldn't come, and he scolded himself for hoping to see her. When would he learn?

His cell buzzed, his assistant's name flashing across the screen. "Park."

"Logan? Hey, it's Chloe."

Logan smiled. "I know. Your name showed on the screen." Chloe had been his assistant for a year and yet still she walked on eggshells around him, petrified he would fire her for talking too much or not talking enough or any one of a thousand reasons she gave him over the year. The truth was he liked her, despite her spazzy ways.

A red convertible darted in front of him, cutting him off and nearly crashing into the car in the lane beside him before switching back to its original lane. "Watch out!" he called, tossing his hands as though the car could see him.

"What?"

"Not you. This idiot driver that nearly caused a pile up on I-75."

"Oh. Well, be careful. And the partners asked when you'll get here. They want to discuss the Maple Cove acquisition."

His shoulders tensed up despite his effort to remain calm. "Tell them I'll be there in an hour. But I need you to pull some things for me. I'll be working remotely for the next few weeks to make sure everything's in order."

"Remotely? You mean at the bed-and-breakfast?"

The idea edged dangerously close to crazy, but Logan needed a comfortable place to work, and what better place than the bed-and-breakfast, so he could make sure there were no surprises for the company. And, okay, maybe he wanted to watch out for Savannah. He sensed yesterday that her brother and sister wouldn't step up, and someone had to be there for her. Now that Will was gone, it was his job, he told himself. Just like it was his job to do all the other things Will couldn't do.

"Yeah. I'll be there for two weeks." Then he rattled off to Chloe all the things he needed—files he wanted transferred to the main server so he could access them remotely. Floor plans of the bed-and-breakfast. Land details. Sales figures for the past five years. And then figures for comparable establishments in the South. Part of what had made him so successful in such a short amount of time was his ability to not only find solid investments, but to figure out what they needed to turn profit.

Maybe Maple's bed-and-breakfast needed a new chef, a specialty dessert menu, or a backyard patio with a seating area overlooking the gardens. The most popular B and B's across the South all had a singular thing that defined them. Some were food related, some were activity related, but they all had something, and Logan felt sure Maple's lack of focus could be the reason for the steady sales decline over the last few years. Staying there would allow him to see its virtues and its flaws. And he saw no harm getting a little face time with its current owner while he scouted out the place.

He hung up with Chloe and hit the radio, flipping from station to station in search of something that would ease the nervousness in his gut. Finally, "Take it to the Limit" by the Eagles came on, and Logan's hand dropped from the control on his steering wheel, his thoughts on Savannah and how different his life could have been if he'd just asked her out first. There would never have been a fight between him and Will during their Afghanistan deployment. Hell, he might not have joined at all. And then instead of helping a company buy the bed-and-breakfast, he would be helping Savannah save it. Like he wanted to now—but Hartridge and Long was too invested, the partners too set on their goal. There was no pulling out, even if he wanted to. And did he want to? Would he really jeopardize his career for a woman who could barely stand him?

Yes.

The problem was, he could risk everything and it might not change a thing. The bed-and-breakfast would still sell to the highest bidder, Savannah would be no closer to being his, and he would have failed Will.

He parked in the garage and made his way into Hartridge and Long's office in the Queen building in Dunwoody with every bit of the composure he always had on the job. It was something the partners had mentioned in his last review—that nothing shook him. They didn't understand that after what he had experienced during his deployments, nothing in the business world, or even the civilian world, *could* shake him. Well, nothing except a certain feisty strawberry blonde.

Chloe stood the moment she saw him, fidgeting with the bangles around her wrist, like always. Her jet black hair was styled in its usual bob, her eyes heavily lined, something that reminded him so much of his mother he had almost turned her away after the interview. But then he told himself that not all women who wore eyeliner were also horrible people, so he took a chance.

"I have everything ready for you," she said, greeting him. "Printouts are on your desk in case you need them. The files are all on the server under your name and today's date. Bob and Alan asked to see you as soon as you arrived."

Logan nodded. "Thanks." Then he continued into his

office, shutting the door quietly behind him, needing a moment to breathe before going in to meet with the partners. Logan liked them, respected them, but he knew his job was only as secure as his latest sale. A month away from a promotion and a month away from losing his job. The instability had at first been a thrill, but now it was...tiring.

Staring out his office window at the outstretched city, he felt cramped. Though his townhouse served its purpose, he had forgotten what a slow life was like, and now that he had visited Maple, he found himself itching to return. Even if a part of that itch was his desire to see Savannah again.

He sat in his chair and, with reluctance, opened the top desk drawer, taking out the photo he kept stashed there for especially troubling days. It was the same photo he'd taken with him to Afghanistan. Just the sight of it gave him strength.

The photo was from Homecoming, everyone around the senior float, Savannah dead center, that wide smile on her face that looked only a breath away from laughter. He couldn't remember where Will had been when he took the photo, but Logan felt guiltily glad he wasn't in it. Logan couldn't imagine looking at Savannah the way he did now with Will standing beside her, his arm draped around her shoulders.

God, what was wrong with him? Will deserved to have a woman like Savannah, not him. Especially not now.

"Logan?" Chloe peeked inside his door, as nervous as ever.

"Going now."

He dropped the photo back into his desk and went down the hall to the double doors that led to Alan's office. A large mahogany desk sat against the left wall, a round table with four chairs against the right. Floor to ceiling windows lined the wall across from the door, and though Logan felt he was lucky to have a window at all, he could get lost in an office like this, staring outside, his mind churning away. Though lately all his mind did was wonder *what if.*

"Good to see you, Logan," Bill said, always the nicer of the two. His hair seemed to gray more each time Logan saw him. His black suit and white dress shirt were the same brand and style he wore every day. "How's your golf game?"

Logan grinned. "As abysmal as ever, which I imagine means you want to play me sometime."

Bill laughed, causing his rather round stomach to jiggle. "The mediocre always want to team with the novice. Makes us feel better about our plainness."

Alan, never one for small talk, or golf, cleared his throat and pushed his small wire frame glasses higher on the bridge of his nose then peered over them at Logan. The light from above shined off his nearly bald head, and not for the first time, Logan had to look away to keep from laughing. He would have said the office decorator should have planned for that, but the decorator was Alan's wife, and Logan thought maybe she *did* plan for it and was laughing to herself somewhere in their monstrosity of a home.

"How's Maple Cove?" Alan asked finally.

"Clean," Logan answered simply, then seeing the joke pass Alan without a smirk, he continued. "The new owners are there now, likely evaluating how far behind they are on the mortgage."

"I thought you said they wouldn't want the place? That we could easily purchase without issue?"

Logan nodded. "I still think it's possible, but they just lost their mother. There are obviously emotional ties to the place. None of the children have expressed interest in taking over, but I feel I should stay around for a few weeks just to feel things out. I'd also like to know what sort of repairs are needed before we buy it."

"Are you suggesting you stay on the premises?"

Leaning back in his chair, Logan noticed the old painting hanging behind Alan's desk—a Revolutionary War era image of a man standing tall and arrogant against the world. Very Alan.

"I think it's the best way for me to scope out any issues."

Bill reached for his coffee and laughed again. "Goodness, man, you are heartless. But I'm glad you work for us and not a competitor. Stay until the deal is done. We don't want any issues."

"I'll take care of it."

Logan stepped into his townhome, set his keys on the kitchen key holder, and peered around. Had his home always looked so…beige? The walls, the furniture, even the few wall hangings were all the same bland shade, and as Logan walked upstairs to his room to pack, he realized that the color wasn't he only reason his apartment felt empty. It *was* empty. Few people had ever stepped foot inside, and even fewer had been there more than once.

He'd always told himself that he was a private person, but really he was afraid to let anyone in. In his twenty-eight years, he'd allowed exactly two people to crack through his hard exterior. One was dead and the other may never speak to him again once this deal was final. And so he'd hired someone to decorate his home, to paint it, to make it easy to sell should he decide to leave. But never along the way did he realize how lonely his home felt—or how lonely he felt inside it.

With new energy, he set to packing, eager to return to Maple, where he may not be welcome, but he never once felt lonely.

Staring at her mama's closet, Savannah wondered how one chose the last outfit a person would wear. Whether to go with a dress—which her mama hated—or jeans, which she loved. Whether to go full suit or blouse and slacks. Memories came back of her and Leigh playing in the large walk-in closet, a mess of shoes scattered on the floor. How had they gone from that moment of bliss to this? How could a single space hold both joy and sadness?

She didn't know. What Savannah did know was that she, herself, would be cremated. The meeting with Brown's Funeral Home was enough to cement that decision. Talk of the service itself, the songs to play during the receiving of friends. The casket. Dear God, the casket.

Choosing the casket her mama would lay in forever broke her heart in two. She stood there listening as they went over the options and all Savannah could think was that none of it was good enough. Not the casket. Not the service. Not the songs. And certainly not the dress or outfit or suit.

"Tell me what to do, Mama." Savannah asked into the

open. "Help me. Guide me. Boss me around and tell me I'm being a foolish child, but please tell me something, because I can't do this."

She pressed her face into her hands, just as there was a loud smack from the closet. She jerked back to see a pair of dark jeans on the floor. Her gaze lifted to the top of the closet where'd they had been moments before. Jesus C and Mary of loving God.

"Mama?" she asked, edging slowly into the closet.

A voice from behind her said, "Who the hell are you talking to?" Savannah jumped back, dropping the jeans, only to find Leigh staring at her like she was a crazy person. In her defense, the jeans had just dropped out of thin air.

"Savannah?"

"What?"

"You're shaking."

She stared down at her hands to find the traitors rattling like half-dead leaves in the wind. "I'm fine. I figured out Mama's outfit."

Leigh's eyebrow lifted. "Okay. Well, where is it?"

With only a moment's hesitation, Savannah bent down and picked up the jeans. "These. But I'll need a top of some sort." She turned back to the closet. "Maybe I should get her something new."

"You're joking."

"Well, I just thought Betsy might have something nice that would—"

"We are not burying Mama in *jeans*. That's... What's the matter with you? This is her *funeral*. You don't bury a person in jeans. You put them in a stylish suit or dress and lots of makeup. What you don't do is put them in jeans and a T-shirt and call it a day. This is Mama. Don't you care what she looks like? Don't you—"

Savannah scowled. "Right. Because you and Jack were at Brown's with me today. Stood right there offering your help and opinion as I selected her casket. As I chose her music. Now suddenly you're giving out opinions like candy on Halloween?" Taking a step back to calm her nerves, she focused on the closet. Then it occurred to her that she had no idea where Leigh had been earlier that day. Or where she'd run off to yesterday. "Where were you, anyway?"

Leigh became very interested in a loose string at the edge of her shirt. "Um, I was at the hardware store picking up a hammer and some screws."

"Since when do you spend so much time at the hardware store? And you don't hammer screws."

"You could!"

"You could not!"

Jack walked in then, chewing gum in the most obnoxious way imaginable. "Hey, Savannah, we need you—"

She tossed her hands up. "Can't any of you do anything for yourselves?" she shouted.

He took a step back, then looked at Leigh for help, but she was still glaring at Savannah.

"Mama's not wearing jeans. Figure out something else."

"You figure it out," Savannah said before sweeping from the room, Jack on her heels.

"Look, I know you're having a moment, but we have—"

They reached the bottom of the steps, and she whirled on him. "I don't give a flying shit what you need."

The sound of someone clearing his throat behind her and Jack's widened eyes had Savannah slowly turning around, the hairs on the back of her neck raised like they knew whatever she was about to see was going to bring her enough embarrassment for a lifetime. Sure enough, she stared straight into the wrinkled face of Pastor Parkins, his mouth set in a grim line as he ran a hand over his balding head.

"Oh my God, I— No, not *oh my God*, like *God*, God. It's...I..." Just then the screen door opened and Logan walked in, a wide grin on his face. "Jesus Christ," Savannah said, then her gaze snapped back to the pastor, both their faces successfully red now.

"I'm just going to set my service notes on the desk here and leave you to it." He turned to go, Savannah still begging him for forgiveness and assuring him she'd pray for her sins.

"Fantastic work, Savannah. We'll be lucky if we're ever allowed in church again," Jack said as he threw his gum in the trash and grabbed a Hershey's kiss from the bowl on the front desk.

"Like you've once stepped foot in church since you left."

Then she spun to face the new thorn in her side, who was leaning ever so casually against the doorjamb, arms crossed over his impeccably toned chest. He wore faded jeans and a white Ralph Lauren polo shirt that looked far too good on him for the mood she was in.

"Did the devil send you here to further test my good girl image? Because I'm thinking that went out the door with the pastor."

Logan smirked. "Nah. Despite appearances, you lost that good girl card in ninth grade when you snuck into an R rated movie when you were supposed to be seeing the G rated one."

"Who told you—never mind." Savannah straightened

her posture, which had gone slack after back-to-back confrontations. She didn't know where Leigh had gone. Likely hiding all of Mama's jeans. "What are you doing here?"

With a sidelong look to Jack, he walked over to the front desk and pressed the bell once, sending a *jingle, jingle* into the air. "I'm here for a room."

"Is that supposed to be funny?"

"Not at all. I told you I was in town on business. I'm not supposed to leave until this is all wrapped up, and there aren't too many places available to stay in town. Figured after yesterday you had plenty of rooms to spare, so here I am." He flashed his ultra white teeth, and Savannah's scowl deepened.

"You're not staying here."

"Yes I am."

"No. You're not. This is my bed-and-breakfast and I say who stays."

Jack walked over and placed a hand on Logan's shoulder in support. "Wait just a second. This isn't *your* bed-and-breakfast. It's all of ours, and Logan's a friend of mine. He can stay."

"He's not your friend."

"You don't say who's my friend or not."

Good God, she was dealing with five-year-olds. Then she realized she'd yet again used God's name in vain and cringed. Glancing up, she said a little "sorry," then returned her attention to the creature in front of her, who was now biting his lip to keep from laughing.

"Struggling there?" he asked.

"*No.*"

"Why are you so angry with Logan anyway?" Jack asked,

causing Logan's gaze to find the floor.

Savannah's mind went right back to that day—her standing on his front steps, desperate to see him, and his piece of crap father coming out to tell her Logan had left. Without a single note or text or word of good-bye. He just left. She'd thought they were...well, she didn't know what they were, but certainly more than people who left without saying anything.

She swallowed down her hurt pride and lifted her chin a touch. "I'm not angry at him. I just don't want him here."

"Well, too bad. He's staying." Jack unlocked the cabinet behind them and pulled out a key. "Second floor, third door on the right. Directly across from Savannah."

Chapter Five

Logan came out of his room an hour later to go into town for dinner, eager to take in every detail of the bed-and-breakfast.

Photos of events around town hung on the wallpapered walls of the second floor. Kids bobbing for apples during the summer craft fair. A band playing at the spring fair. All of Maple's history rested on these walls, and though Logan no longer lived there, he felt a sense of pride as he took in the photos. For all their faults and gossiping natures, Maple's citizens were a happy bunch.

Feeling like a traitor for leaving, he dipped his head and started for the stairs, only to find Savannah sitting on the fifth step down, her legs stretched across the step, her eyes focused on nothing in particular. It was after six now, and as far as he could tell he was the only one staying at the bed-and-breakfast, though Jim had fixed the water that morning.

Without asking, he squatted down and sat a few steps

above her. Immediately, that fresh-from-the-dryer warmth he felt whenever he was around her hit him, sinking into his tired muscles and reminding him of easier days. "What is it, Anna?"

"It's…never mind. Nothing."

"You can tell me."

She pulled her knees into her chest and turned to look at him. "Actually, I can't. You're the enemy."

"I'm a lot of things, but I'm not the enemy and you know it. Tell me what's bothering you."

She blinked, hesitating, then finally said, "I'm messing everything up."

"What? No you're not. You're doing great."

She released a sarcastic laugh. "I chose a cherry casket, but Jack told me Mama hates cherry. Then I chose jeans for her outfit and Leigh practically crucified me. I'm trying so hard to get it all right, and I'm failing at each turn. They're counting on me and I'm failing." She swiped a lone tear from her cheek and pushed her legs back across the step. "I just want to stand up there tomorrow and make Mama proud, but I'm afraid that I'll do nothing but fall to my knees." She glanced up at him again, her expression full of pain. "Do you ever feel like you might collapse if you stop and think for too long?" Swiping another tear, she laughed, the sound so far from her real laugh it nearly broke his heart. "I'm sure you have no idea what I'm talking about."

Logan leaned back against the wall and released a breath. "Sometimes I lay awake at night and wonder if you can die from expectation and burden. If the weight finally becomes too much to carry and you just…die."

"Logan?"

He found her eyes again and saw the question on the tip of her tongue. The question he refused to answer, even to himself, though he'd long since known the response. For years now, he told himself he'd call her and explain, and now here she was, no one around, the crickets outside the only sound, but he couldn't say it. The truth was too cowardly to admit. So instead, he stepped over her and reached out for her hand. "Let's get some dinner."

"Together? But I don't like you right now."

A grin played at his lips, but he didn't want her to think he was laughing at her, so he pushed it away. "I know. Maybe put that aside in the name of hunger. What do you say? You're hungry, let's eat."

"I don't want to go out like this. And besides…everyone'll talk."

Logan knew she meant that she didn't want to be seen alone with him, and though it stung a little that she would always be Will's girl, he ignored it. She needed him even if her pride refused to admit it.

"We don't have to leave. I'll cook you something from the kitchen."

"You cook?"

He nodded. "One of the men in my platoon liked to cook. Taught me a thing or two." When she didn't respond after a moment, he added, "It's just a meal, Anna. Basic stuff."

"Yeah, I guess you're right." She stood, and it took everything in him to not reach for her hand, to comfort her and let her know she wasn't alone. Not as long as he was alive. But instead, he walked quietly behind her.

"What was it like?" she asked as they went down the long hall and through the white swinging door to the kitchen. The bed-and-breakfast had been renovated since the last time Logan was there, but he could still sense Jane Hale in the kitchen, apron around her.

Logan stalled in answering the question and went for the double fridge, opening the doors to find containers of sliced chicken, steak, fish…the works. He decided on fajitas, knowing Savannah had always been a big fan of Mexican food. Then he realized maybe that, like so many other things, had changed.

"Fajitas okay?" he asked, tossing a green pepper into the air and catching it easily.

A flicker of a smile crossed her lips, and his eyes dropped to her mouth, curious how to make it happen again. "I love Mexican food."

His gaze held hers, his heart a noticeable presence in his chest. "I remember."

Savannah cleared her throat then asked, "Do you not like to talk about your time in the service?"

The kitchen was too quiet, no sound but the occasional breeze or cricket or tree limb rustling against a window. Nothing to distract him from the question. The truth was, Logan felt significant pride for his time in the army, but he'd never known true fear before then, and for a man to talk about fear was like asking him to break off his arm without blinking.

"I wasn't there when it happened," he said to her, sure what she really wanted to know was how Will had died. They'd had this conversation before, but he knew first hand that there were complex things in life you wanted to hear again and again in hopes of finding a missing detail that would help it all make sense. But there was no sense in a nineteen-year-old dying in duty. Honor, sure. But sense? It would never come.

"Actually." She pushed onto the counter top, her legs swinging a touch, bringing back memories that made his chest ache with longing. "I was wondering about...before. Can you tell me how it was for you?"

He walked past her, his arm grazing her knee, and they both stilled. Her legs stopped swinging and his breath caught. It had always been this way—the spark between them ready to rage at a moment's notice—but he'd thought it might have gone away by now, age diminishing its intensity. He was wrong.

Clearing his throat, he went to work on the food. "You feel a bond unlike anything you've ever felt before. The men and women in your unit have your back in the worst and best situations of your day. You learn to depend on each other, laugh with each other. That part I loved."

"But the other part?"

Logan thought of his second deployment, when he went to Iraq, and the voice in the back of his head that said he could be walking and get blown away, gone before he had a chance to run. Knowing not everyone would make it back. The fear would be so real he'd have no choice but to tuck it into the back of his mind, because if he succumbed to it he'd come back to the States in a casket instead of on his feet.

And then he'd hear someone in his unit was shot, and he'd say a silent prayer that it wasn't Kip or Mark or Blue, someone he'd grown close to, and then he'd realize that there was no one he'd volunteer for the dead card. Then it would all start again the next day, and the next, and the next. But people didn't want to hear the bad stuff.

"I was glad to offer what I could for my country."

Savannah cocked her head, her eyes studying him as he chopped up onions and red and green peppers, the skillet already sizzling away on the stovetop beside him. "Serving is an amazing thing. What you did was an amazing thing."

His eyes lifted, then he shrugged. "There was a time I thought so, when the bravery was enough to make me feel like a man. But those ideals are replaced with something more when you see a man die."

They fell into silence, listening to the chicken and vegetables sauté, when she said, "Why weren't you with him?"

And there it was, the question he didn't want to answer. "They separated our unit. One platoon went one way, one the other." And they'd just had a fight about her, so Logan had demanded to go with the other platoon. He should be in the ground right now, just like Will. For months after, the what-ifs would drive him to the bottom of more bottles than he could count, but even if he'd been with Will, he couldn't have saved him. Still, understanding and accepting were not at all the same things.

"Do you ever miss it? The army?"

Logan went to the pantry and pulled out some tortillas and chips, then smiled at the avocado and cilantro he found in the refrigerator. He began mixing the two with a few other seasonings to make a quick guacamole because he knew Savannah loved it. Then returning to the island where she sat, he set out the chips and guacamole, sliding them toward her. "I miss parts of it. There's something reassuring about having a purpose. No matter what I did, each day I knew my job, and therefore my life had meaning. The civilian world never provides that same assurance."

"No, it doesn't." Her face dropped and Logan went for

the fridge again to grab a chilled bottle of wine. Uncorking it and grabbing two glasses, he nodded for her to join him at the small two-person table just outside the French doors of the kitchen. She followed and he brought out the food on bright red and brown serving plates that looked very Spanish, sure she'd get a kick out of it.

"I feel like I'm at a restaurant now. Who knew you were the real thing, Logan Park," she said, nodding to the plates.

"Baby, it doesn't get more real than me."

"No…it doesn't." Their eyes held and Savannah cleared her throat, took a long sip of her wine, then set it down and returned her gaze to his.

"So what's Boston Savannah like?" Logan asked, truly curious.

She laughed. "Boring. I work in consulting and it's good, but I work long hours and my friends are less friends and more colleagues, so all we talk about is work."

He nodded, watching as she took a bite of the food. Then that bite led to another bite and another.

"Wow, I had no idea you could cook. This is amazing."

"I try."

"Well color me impressed."

Logan smiled, pleased with her compliments. "Thanks. But the job—you love it?"

She hesitated. "Define love."

"Not this man. But you seem to like the B and B."

At that she laughed loudly, the sound so rich all he could do was stare. "I'm lost here. I feel like I can't make my brain work, and I make more mistakes than successes. It's exhausting. All I want to do is fix everything and everybody."

"Things, sure," Logan said around a bite. "But you can't

fix people, Anna. They have to fix themselves."

"Maybe. But if I can just get through this funeral and get this place running again, then my family will be okay."

He took a sip of his wine, wishing he'd grabbed a beer for himself instead. Wine was never his drink, too fruity and feminine. He liked the taste of it on a woman's lips, but otherwise he liked to crack open a can and drink the way men were meant to drink. "And if you can't?"

"Then my family falls apart."

"They're stronger than you think."

Her bottom lip trembled as tears burned her eyes. "You think so?"

"They're a part of you. I know so." Savannah looked away, fighting a yawn, and he stood up. "Go on to bed. Get some rest. I'll clean up."

"No, I can help."

He shook his head. "Nah, you've got enough to deal with."

She held his gaze, and he thought she wanted to say something more, but instead she pushed her chair out and placed her napkin on her plate. "Thank you for this. It helped. A lot."

"I'm glad."

Logan cleaned up and then went to bed that night wondering when people tossed burdens onto their backs. Did it land there when they were kids along with their backpacks full of books and pencils and notepads? Or did they inherit it from their parents as they aged, a transfer from generation to generation. He wasn't sure, but one thing he did know—Jane Hale's funeral was in less than two days and whether Savannah thought she needed him or not, he would help her carry her burden.

Chapter Six

Savannah watched as her brother and sister walked ahead of her down the center aisle of the funeral home's chapel, her head as straight as a pin, her chin high. She feared if she dropped it even an inch she'd never be able to lift it again.

People packed into all of the pews, with most of Maple Cove in attendance and many travelling in from out of town to pay their respects to a woman whose smile alone made everything just a little bit easier. Savannah wished her mama could see it now.

The receiving had been painful, but formulaic, and she'd been thankful Will's parents were out of town and couldn't make it. They'd called her at the bed-and-breakfast to give their respects and that had been rough enough.

Savannah went through each section of the receiving as though it were another part of her job, pushing aside her feelings and ignoring the tug in her chest at the kind words from those who cared for her mother. She didn't cry or laugh or show any emotion at all, beyond the small smile that tugged at her lips when she saw her mama in the casket for the first time. Jane Hale wore a lovely blouse and an even lovelier necklace, but from the waist down, out of view, she was dressed in the jeans she'd dropped on Savannah.

No one would know—including Leigh. But Savannah couldn't get the sound of those jeans falling down from her mama's closet out of her head. Signs might be a silly woman's way of seeing the world, but in times of death, people clung to whatever helped them cope. So Jane Hale would forever rest in jeans.

One piece of the funeral arrangements over, Savannah went into today knowing this would be the hardest to get through. A part of her wanted to stay home, claim she'd taken ill with a stomach flu, and wallow in her tears and misery. But Leigh and Jack needed her, so there she was, chin high as she walked down the aisle after them, several heads turning as though it were her wedding day.

Her wedding day.

The thought hit her square in the chest, choking her before she could stop it. Neither of her parents would see her get married. Her daddy would not walk her down the aisle. Her mama would not press a tissue to the corners of her eyes and tell Savannah she looked beautiful. Her mama would never hold her first-born grandchild, never smile with fresh tears at the addition to their family legacy. Nothing would have made her mama happier, but she would never see it. She would never see any of it.

Oh God.

Her chin dipped a half-inch, no more, but the effect on the rest of her body was immediate. Savannah felt herself crumbling, her shoulders drooping, her stomach clenching, her legs buckling.

No, stand. Stand!

By some grace, her eyes connected with the person standing in the pew closest to her, and she almost cried with relief. Logan. It seemed fitting that out of everyone, he was the lighthouse guiding her home. She drew a breath, and he nodded to her, assuring her that she could do this. And if she couldn't, then he'd be there to catch her. It was no wonder she'd fallen in love with him all those years ago.

The sureness in his gaze guided her the last few steps to the front pew, beside her brother and sister. She felt his stare on her back like a caress, and she wished he were beside her, all the complications of their relationship erased if only for that day. She imagined his hand in hers, a reminder that she would survive this. No one died from the death of someone else. But in that moment, Savannah questioned if the ache in her heart could stop it from beating, unable to take the pain.

The music she'd selected continued to play as others came in and filled up the available seats, some standing in the back after there were no free spaces to sit. She smiled at the crowd, touched that they cared enough about her mother to attend.

Then the song switched and the one song Savannah had intentionally left off the list began to play.

Amazing Grace how sweet the sound…

No, not this song. Anything but this song. Savannah gripped the back of the pew in front of her, and suddenly she was six-years old again, tears on her cheek as a summer thunderstorm beat against the house, rattling the windows. Her mother had drifted into her room like an angel and wrapped her warm arms around her, drying her tears while she sang "Amazing Grace" her words drowning out the storm as she stroked her hair until Savannah fell fast asleep again.

Leigh broke down beside her, likely recounting a similar memory of her own, and Jack held her to him, their heads close as they consoled one another, Savannah alone beside them. Standing strong for them. But she didn't feel strong. Her hands trembled on the pew in front of her and her legs shook so violently she wondered how she stood at all. And then she heard Leigh whisper, "I miss her," and Savannah's grasp slipped, her body no longer willing to hold on as the first tear fell, allowing the dam to break.

Logan watched Jack's arms wrap around Leigh, holding her up as Pastor Parkins walked to the podium at the front of the chapel. Which left Savannah there beside them, standing tall, her head too high, her posture too tight. She was about to lose it, her worst fear coming true. But the problem was she didn't realize that was okay. It was okay to melt right now, to fall apart. No one would judge her. No one would view her as weak.

Her hands tightened on the pew in front of her and her head dipped, like the weight of the whole world rested on her shoulders, and Logan couldn't handle it anymore.

Without a word, he slipped out of his pew and into hers to stand beside her, letting his strength be hers. Savannah whispered a small thanks to him, her lips quivering as her sister's cries became louder, and she shook her head, anger in her eyes. But he knew this anger wasn't for him. She was angry at the tears on her cheeks. Angry at her brother and sister. Angry at a world that would take her mother. She gritted her teeth and drew a sharp breath, trying harder to rein in her tears. He wanted to tell her to stop fighting it, to allow the grief to overcome her. There was no fighting it here. Not now, when her heart didn't know how to cope.

Reaching into his pocket, Logan pulled out a handkerchief and gently dried her cheeks so she didn't have to lose her grip on the pew, on her world, and then placed his hand over hers, refusing to let go.

"Logan…"

"You carry everyone's weight," he whispered. "For today, let me carry yours."

She flipped her hand, threading her fingers with his, and he switched hands so his right held her left and then slipped his arm over her shoulders, pulling her to him.

Without thinking, he dropped a kiss on the top of her head, taking in the floral scent of her shampoo, and closed his eyes for a moment, remembering them in a similar embrace after Will's funeral.

But they hadn't been in front of half the town then. They'd been out on the swing at Cross Creek Plantation, the same place he'd found her when he delivered the news about Will's death. Somehow that swing had become their safe place, and before long they'd silently agreed to meet there everyday. Sometimes they would do nothing but stare at the small lake in front of them. Other times they'd lie out in the grass and talk about what they'd do if they could do anything, where they'd go, who they'd be.

It was a quiet night when their friendship shifted quickly

into something more. He'd turned to laugh at something she'd said, but the expression on her face wasn't full of humor. The change was so small that if he'd not been paying attention he might have missed it. But he was—he'd been watching for weeks, every single day of his time back home, knowing any day he'd leave for his second deployment, yanked back to his other life, the other version of himself, nothing but a photo of her to keep him safe and warm at night. Without pause, he reached for her hand, tracing the lines of her palm, his eyes never leaving hers.

Hours passed before they finally let go, and he knew exactly what he'd see on her face, but that didn't stop the pain from slicing through his gut as he took it in—regret.

He'd been a fool to ever hope for something more with Savannah, but hope was a stupid thing that refused to listen to good sense. So he tucked away his pride and took her home, refusing to look at her. He didn't want to see the regret in her eyes again.

And then the storm rolled in—in more ways than one.

Two days later, he gave her an out—he left for Iraq. No good-bye, no explanation. He allowed her to hate him instead of love him. It was the second hardest thing he'd ever done in his life, but at the same time, it was the right thing to do. That part he knew.

Now, years later, but he couldn't help wonder what would have happened if he'd stayed, talked, tried. Would they be together now? Married? Children? Would he holding his wife as she cried instead of this woman who was almost a stranger to him? He didn't know.

The service ended and Logan squeezed Savannah's shoulder, expecting her to pull away. Instead, she gripped his hand tighter. "Will you…?"

Her voice hitched, and he nodded. "Whatever you need."

She walked out hand-in-hand with him, not arguing when he guided her to his truck and helped her inside. Then they led the family procession, behind the hearse and cop car, her staring out the back window, a solemn look on her face.

"What are you doing?" Logan asked after several minutes.

She turned around, a small smile on her face. "I'm counting cars. It's nice to see so many people. Mama was loved."

Logan reached for her hand. "She was."

"Thank you. For the service. For this. For everything." She leveled her gaze on him, her eyes still red and puffy from crying, but damn if she wasn't as beautiful as ever.

He wanted to say he'd do anything for her, be anywhere, walk through fire, but those weren't things she needed to hear just then. So instead, he accepted her gratitude with a single nod and gently stroked her hand with his thumb as he drove her to the burial. For now, that was enough for him.

Chapter Seven

It took Savannah a week to organize things at the bed-and-breakfast enough to open it back up for business. The water was one thing, but as she walked from room to room, each floor, each section, she found a laundry list of things that needed fixing. None of that included the business of the financials, which Savannah had finally mustered up the courage to tackle, praying her mama hadn't been the one she'd learned her spending habits from.

She sat down at the desk in her parents' office and pulled out the file their accountant Frank had given her. A strange look had crossed his face when he'd passed it over, like he was handing her a mouse in a trap, glad to see it off his property.

Keeping the place closed for a week had been a risk, but Logan paid her every day as if it were his last, only to book another day and then another. And though at first she'd been angry to see him staying at the bed-and-breakfast, now it was a relief to have a friendly face around.

Opening the file, Savannah read through the numbers, her eyebrows threading together with each line until she reached the very red number at the end. She pushed out of the cracked leather chair and stood over the paperwork, sure she wasn't reading it correctly. But there it was, plain as day, screaming at her that she didn't need glasses after all.

The bed-and-breakfast was four months behind in its mortgage, and if she didn't bring it current in the next twenty-five days, the house would go into foreclosure.

Her heart sped up as she read the words again and again. Foreclosure. So Logan's employer didn't just want to buy the bed-and-breakfast. They planned to swoop in and get it for a giant discount once the house foreclosed. The jerks!

She thought of trying to sell the place and felt her heart drop. The Hales had always owned the bed-and-breakfast. It'd been in their family for three generations. What had happened? Yes, Jane Hale was bad with money, but this?

She picked up the phone in the office and dialed their accountant then, growing frustrated, packed up all the paperwork and slid back into her flip-flops, deciding she'd just walk down to Frank's office instead.

Flying out of the room, she narrowly missed Logan, whose friendly face was looking less and less friendly to her by the second. "You didn't tell me you were some bottom-feeder wanting to snatch the place once we lost it."

He shook his head. "What?" Then his gaze landed on the folder with a thousand papers sticking out in a thousand different directions. "It isn't like that. We should talk about this."

"What is there to talk about? Is that why you're here?

To spy on things? See what you're getting?"

When he didn't answer, she stormed past him.

"Wait, let me—"

She spun around. "Explain? Is there an explanation? Really? 'Cause I don't think there is. You know, every time I think I can count on you, every time I let my guard down, you toss me right back to the ground. What did I ever do to make you hate me so much? Was it Will? Jealousy? Because I'll tell you something, Logan Park, never once did I hate you. And never in my life would I kick you when you were already at your lowest. I just lost my mama and now you're here to take the one thing that meant the most to her. I want you out of here. Now."

The sky turned dark overhead, matching Savannah's mood as she marched down the cobblestone road and straight toward Frank's office. She couldn't believe Logan. Couldn't believe she'd been so stupid. Again! How was it possible that one man could weasel his way into her heart again and again without her learning?

Well, no more.

She tore into Cooke Accounting, ignoring the looks from Louisa, Frank's admin, seated at the small front desk, eating a jelly donut by the looks of the sticky stuff on her chin and fingertips.

"Is he here?" Savannah asked. Then without waiting for an answer she marched down the hall and tossed open the last door on the right to find the small old man behind his desk, his glasses jumping to his forehead as he jumped at her intrusion.

"Ms. Hale? What on earth?"

"Why didn't you tell me the bed-and-breakfast was in

the red? Did you want to wait until it foreclosed? I should have gotten a call the moment I came to town."

"I thought you needed to deal with your mama's death. I didn't want to—"

"You let me close it down for a week! I could have helped get it back up."

Frank threaded his fingers together and peered at her like she was a lost puppy who'd never had a home to begin with. "I don't think there's anything that can be done at this point. Your mother tried to refinance and—"

"Well, as you can plainly see, I'm not my mama."

He straightened. "But Jane said you had no interest in taking over the bed-and-breakfast. That none of you did. Besides, you have no idea how to run one."

"Yeah, well, everybody's got to start somewhere."

Savannah walked out and slammed the door, fuming. Then, remembering that she still needed him to actually *be* her accountant, she walked back in, an apologetic smile on her face. "Thank you for your time," she said, then closed the door quietly and nodded to Louisa before setting out down the sidewalk, crossing over to Southern Sandwich for some food and coffee. She needed nourishment if she hoped to save her family's business.

As always, Southern Sandwich brimmed with people, the shop still a favorite in the town. The walls were all lined with photos—some old, some new. Some from Maple, and some from events in the South. Light blue booths lined one wall, and a dozen four-chair tables occupied the rest of the open space, blue- and white-checkered print on the tablecloths. From the look to the smell, the sandwich shop oozed everything Southern.

Savannah smiled as Mrs. Gray, the shop owner, came over and patted Savannah's hand. She wore a white dress with a bright red apron, the words "Life never brings a baker lemons. Only lemon cake" in swirling yellow across the top. Her dark, curly hair was pinned into a bun, like always, and her face bore not a trace of makeup. With a glow like hers, she never needed it.

"Have whatever you like, honey. On the house."

"Oh, that's not—"

"It's what Jane would have done for my girls."

Savannah sighed. Mrs. Gray was right. Jane would have given anyone who needed it a free stay at the bed-and-breakfast, which was perhaps what landed it in such financial ruin.

With a hug and a thank-you, Savannah slid into a table in the back corner and spread out the financials again, eager to see what she could do, but her eyes went straight to the giant red number. There should be a sticky note of warning on this folder—*enter at your own risk, could cause possible heart attack or prolonged weeping.*

She had a third of the money they needed in savings, but how could she get the rest? Leigh or Jack, maybe. Certainly Jack would have money. Unless he, like Savannah, had inherited their mother's spending habits and was as broke as the rest of them.

"Coffee?"

Savannah nodded to Mrs. Gray. "Thank you. And maybe just a ham and cheese croissant?"

"Coming up," Mrs. Gray said, smiling, then her gaze locked on the wall beside Savannah. "Fitting table."

Savannah's eyes lifted to the wall, and her chest clenched

tight at the framed photo beside her. Why didn't she notice it before?

Will and Logan stood in their uniforms, arms draped around each other's shoulders, giant smiles on their faces. They were polar opposites. Logan was all blond hair and impossibly green eyes, set against that golden skin of his. Even in his uniform, he had a rough and wild look about him. Carefree to the extreme, nothing anchoring him in place.

Will was different—fair skin, chocolate hair with just a touch of caramel, blue eyes that were always warm. He was responsible and polished, clearly the result of a proper upbringing. He knew how to speak in a crowd, was well mannered and kind to a fault, which was how he and Logan had become friends in the first place.

Logan's father had been driving drunk and crashed his truck, but he was too gone to even know what had happened. And he certainly couldn't care less that his son was in the car with him. Will's family found ten-year-old Logan walking down the street, a deep gash across his forehead. They took him to the hospital, paid for stitches, and brought him to their house, where he would forever be a family member.

"I can move you if this is too much," Mrs. Gray said, her expression full of concern. She placed a hand on Savannah's shoulder, and the motherly gesture made Savannah ache for her own mother so very badly.

"It's okay." She swallowed and met Mrs. Gray's caring eyes, hoping her own didn't show just how much it hurt to sit here beside Will and Logan, knowing what she felt for each of them…even then.

But she didn't have time to worry about it before her former friends surrounded Mrs. Gray. "We'll make sure she's fine, Mrs. Gray."

"So tell us everything," the blondes said. Savannah quickly closed her paperwork and tried not to come across as frustrated as she felt. No woman should have to run into people from high school when she was at her lowest. It should be a quick pass by, a wave at a traffic light before going on your way. But that wasn't Maple. After all, it only had the two traffic lights, and one remained forever on green.

Savannah laughed uncomfortably. "Oh, not sure what there is to tell."

Brenna pulled out the chair beside Savannah and the other two women took the other chairs. "Well let us fill you in."

Just then Jim walked in, tool belt hanging low around his waist, a swipe of oil or God knew what on his cheek. His dark black hair was cropped short, and his skin had a deep bronze tan from all his work around town. He wore Carhartt cargo pants and a white T-shirt that stretched tight across his muscular frame.

"We'll start with him," Dana said, nodding to Jim.

Doing a double take at Dana, then Jim, Savannah leaned in, allowing herself to get caught up in the gossip, then cursing herself for falling prey to it. She was an adult now! She didn't care who did what with whom! Yet… "Jim? What about him?"

It was Hannah who answered. "Apparently he's been hooking up with someone around town. No one knows who because they've never gone out in public and are very stealthy about the whole thing." She lowered her voice. "Rumor has it he's shacking up with Marlie Blackson."

"*What*?" Savannah recoiled, shaking her head as her

gaze lifted back to Jim, who was now ordering from the to-go counter. "Marlie's married. Jim wouldn't mess around with a married woman."

"How do you know?" Brenna asked, appearing a little too excited to discuss Jim. Like maybe she wished his secret relationship was with her.

"I've known Jim since I was seven years old, when I found him and Jack ripping all the heads off my Barbie dolls. He's Jack's best friend, and he's a good guy."

"Then who?"

Savannah stared between them. "First, how do you know it's someone from town? And second, it's none of our business."

Still, she couldn't help wondering who her old family friend had met.

"Who are you kidding?" Hannah chimed in. "Maple's a small town. Everything's everyone's business, whether we like it or not. Kind of like that thing going on with you and Logan Park. Rumor has it you're making use of all those empty rooms at the B and B."

Savannah choked on her sweet tea, hacking her way through it as she stared wide-eyed at the woman who'd once been her friend, though she couldn't for the life of her remember why. Had they always been like this? It explained why none of them had relationships of their own to worry over.

Mrs. Gray set down a brown bag in front of Savannah, saving her from answering the question. "Your to-go order, honey," Mrs. Gray said, winking at Savannah.

She stood quickly, grabbing the bag and her folder. "Um, thanks. Yeah…I have to go. See you ladies another time."

"We certainly hope so," Dana said.

Then Hannah called out Savannah's name, and she turned to find her smiling a little too sweetly. "If you're not taking advantage of Logan being back in town, then maybe I will." Her eyes twinkled, daring Savannah to stake her claim on Logan. Instead, Savannah gripped the brown bag tighter in her hand.

"Do whatever you like. It doesn't matter to me."

If only she could convince herself of that.

Logan considered packing his things for all of five seconds. But then he thought of all those years of his life spent doing what others told him to do, and he wasn't going. He was sent to Maple for a purpose, and though a part of him was struggling with how he would actually go through with that, he wasn't a quitter. He reminded himself that this was all for Will. Though, he wondered, if Will had worked for Hartsford and Long, like he'd always dreamed of doing, would he have agreed to handle their acquisition of the B and B? Or would he have told them no? Logan couldn't be sure, but he tried to tell himself it wasn't personal. Savannah didn't want the B and B anyway. None of the Hales wanted to run it. Who cared who owned it?

So with that in mind, he wasn't leaving. He decided that if Savannah thought she could kick him out, she'd have to call Travis, Maple's sheriff, to come arrest him, and they both knew Travis would do little more than laugh.

Finishing up a few emails, Logan looked through the files Chloe had saved on the server for him. He scanned the layout of the bed-and-breakfast and then the land. They could definitely expand the back patio. Maybe even do a screened-in siting area to keep the bugs out. They could offer special couple meals out on the patio. Private music, perhaps? Or candlelight? He tapped his pen against the notepad beside his laptop, thinking he'd never be able to create an adequate list of upgrades without doing a full tour of the place.

Resigned, he pushed away from the small wooden desk and peered around the room. There was a queen-size, mahogany wood bed with a white quilt and linens and red throw pillows. The desk chair cushion matched the red pillows, which Logan thought was a nice touch. There was a nightstand to the left of the bed, and to the right a bookshelf with hardcovers stacked in alphabetical order. Then above the desk, attached to the wall, was a forty-two inch TV. The room was cozy, but had its modern touches as well. He wondered if all the rooms were decorated like this one, or if each room was different. There wasn't an easy way to find out without shacking up with another guest or asking Savannah. Somehow the latter seemed the more difficult of the choices.

"Howdy, *neighbor.*"

Logan opened the door to his room to find Leigh leaning against the wall, looking like she'd no sooner trust him than a copperhead. A bright red headband sliced across her ultra-black hair, matching the red of her lipstick. He had no idea why she'd dyed her strawberry blond locks black, but her new dark look matched the glare she shot at him now.

"Leigh. How are you feeling?"

"Don't think I don't know what you're doing." She tapped her head. "Everyone thinks Savannah's the brains of our family, but I'm the silent thinker, and I have all sorts of thoughts about you, Logan Park."

Logan grinned at the use of his full name. Why the Hales chose to call him Logan Park instead of just Logan was beyond him, but he liked it.

"Um, well, glad to hear it. I was just…" Logan pointed to the stairs, but Leigh took a step toward them, blocking him.

"Where are you going?"

"I thought I'd go out on the patio."

"Why?"

Logan started to answer when the room across from Leigh's opened and Jack stepped out. He eyed his sister, then Logan, sensing the tension. "Ignore her." He motioned to the stairs, and he and Logan went down them, Leigh on their heels.

"You realize he's trying to buy the bed-and-breakfast, don't you?"

"So? Let him."

"*What*?" Leigh half shouted at him.

"Actually *I'm* not trying to buy it, my firm is."

Leigh glared at Logan. "And how is that any different?"

"Well—"

"And don't you have an ounce of family loyalty?" she spit out at her brother—literally spitting as she spoke, her anger taking over.

"It's not a matter of family loyalty. We all have lives." Jack crossed his arms, his eyes narrowing. "Well, Savannah and I do. You? I guess you could run it if you'd like, but something tells me you can't afford to. Why not let Park buy it? Who cares?"

Logan could have sworn smoke blew out Leigh's ears. Her fists clenched, and Logan felt it was time to get the hell out of Dodge before he got any more caught up in their sibling squabble.

Pushing through the back French doors, he stepped out onto the deck, walking to the edge and peering around. The deck held two wrought iron tables with ceramic and wrought iron chairs. The deck itself had long since faded, and needed to be pressure-washed and re-stained.

There were four steps that led down to a small patio. Another small three-piece table set was placed just outside the basement door, and then from the patio five or six stepping stones led to the garden around the side of the house, which was by far the best part of the land. Suddenly, Logan understood why the bed-and-breakfast suffered financially. While the inside was fairly well kept and the rooms had their charm, the outside left a lot to be desired.

He pulled out his phone and began snapping pictures of the grounds. The deck. The tables. The overgrown woods. When he turned to take a photo of the deck, a very angry face filled his screen.

"What the hell do you think you're doing?"

Logan couldn't keep the grin from his face as he lowered his phone and tucked it back into his pocket. He'd almost snapped a photo of Savannah just so he could show it to her. Hands on her hips, foot tapping, her adorable face etched in anger—he wondered if she brought that sass to the bedroom, and he found himself wishing he could find out. Just once. Then he'd hide his feelings again and be a good boy.

"Are you going to answer, or keep staring at me with that damn smirk on your face?"

The smirk widened. He couldn't help it. "I thought I'd take a few photos."

"I'm pretty sure that's illegal."

"For guests to take photos of their stay?"

"For lowlife suckers to take research photos on private property. I told you to get out."

Logan cocked his head like he was considering it. "Yeah…I don't think so." He walked around her to the stairs and started down, Savannah rushing after him, so angry now he could almost feel the laser beams from her eyes piercing through his back.

"You can't stay if I tell you to leave."

"Watch me."

She sputtered. "I'll have you arrested."

Logan turned to her, one eyebrow lifted, and she took a step back. "Fine. Travis won't take you in. But I'll have Jack drag your pretty ass right out of here." She crossed her arms.

From the deck, the sound of someone biting an apple had both their heads craning around to see who had invaded their fight.

"Hey, man," Logan called to Jack. "Your sister says you're going to drag my—" He leaned toward Savannah. "What was it you called my ass? Oh, right. Pretty. Didn't realize you'd grown so fond of my ass." He winked at her, causing Savannah to fume even more. Her mouth opened to yell at him, but he raised a hand to stop her. "Do I need to be worried?" he asked Jack, who simply laughed.

"Well, I *am* a pro athlete."

"I heard." Logan scratched his chin. "Though, I was a decorated soldier. Gotta count for something right? Ever shot anybody?" he asked Jack.

Jack laughed. "Point taken. You're on your own, sis. But I'll be sure to watch you try to drag his pretty ass out of here."

"I hate you both," Savannah said, earning a laugh from the men.

The day had started to drift into late afternoon, the hot sun disappearing behind the trees, making the air more comfortable to stand in without melting, but the humidity was still alive and well. He considered asking Savannah if she wanted to go for a swim to cool off that attitude of hers, but he thought that might piss her off even further. Instead, he pointed to the small notepad in her hand.

"What's that?"

"None of your—"

"It's a list of all the stuff to fix around here," Jack called down, causing Savannah to whirl around to him.

"Shut up, or you're next on my blacklist. Blood or not."

Jack threw up his hands, shot Logan a grin, then went back inside.

"Basement doorknob," Logan read from the top of her list. "What's wrong with it?"

"Feel free to find out for yourself," she said, then she disappeared into the gardens, jotting down notes in her little pad the whole way. Logan grinned after her. Her hips swayed as she walked, drawing his gaze to her barely-there shorts and then up her narrow waist to her light blue tank top. The outfit had a very just-thrown-on look, but on Savannah it was sexy as hell.

He turned back to the house, his thoughts on this frustrating woman—the only woman he truly couldn't have and yet the only one he'd truly ever wanted.

Chapter Eight

By the time Savannah completed her list and made it back into the house, she had twenty-three things to fix, none of them especially cheap or easy. The easiest — and hopefully cheapest — had to be the basement door, though the doorknob looked decently new, so she couldn't imagine how she could fix it without calling Jim. He'd already cut her a deal on the water issue, thanks to his long-time friendship with Jack. She couldn't expect another favor.

The house sat quiet, Mrs. Cooke gone home with no guests to attend to, and Leigh and Jack likely in town to eat. She wondered why they could come and go as they liked, eating when they liked, when she was the one running around trying to fix everything.

The thought made her angry, and then she wondered why she was so easily angered all the time. Had she always been this volatile? Surely not.

Her thoughts went to her one and only guest, and she had

her answer. Logan Park was the very definition of annoying. He showed up with his carefree attitude and knowing smirk and threw her world upside down, reminding her very much of the boy she'd once known. Only he didn't look like a boy. No, not a boy at all. With his defined arms and narrow waist, she could only imagine what he looked like behind all those perfectly fitted clothes. And she bet he knew exactly how hot he was, as well as the effect he had on the opposite sex. Damn him.

Cursing herself for her pretty ass comment, she went down the steps to the basement, ordering herself not to be afraid. And to be more careful around Logan, or else she'd reveal just what she truly thought of him. Pretty ass and all.

The door to the basement was closed like always, so she pushed it open and stepped inside. She was about to place her notepad in the doorjamb to prevent it from closing, when she heard someone rushing toward her. "Ahhh!" she screamed and wheeled around, the door slamming shut behind her.

"Fantastic."

Savannah took in Logan, his hands on his hips, his head shaking.

"The door gets caught."

"No kidding," she said. "Why do you think it was on my list? What are you doing down here, anyway?" Her eyes traveled up and down him in an attempt at judgment, but all he did was flash that smirk of his, causing her body to spark and flicker with want. Age had served him well, and with all her pent up emotions—and, okay, recent sexual drought—she was finding it hard to separate her anger from her attraction.

"I tried to fix it, but the door closed on me when I turned around. Then you came in. But now..." He tossed his hand helplessly at the door. "We're stuck."

Savannah grabbed the doorknob and turned, but it just went around, refusing to catch so it could actually open. She pulled the door, jiggled harder, then pulled again, all with no luck. It wouldn't budge. "Ugh!" This wasn't happening. Of all the people to get stuck somewhere with, it had to be Logan. The bottom-feeder who sent her pulse into a frenzied mess. Her bad luck should make it into the *Guinness Book of World Records*.

Walking over to the door that led outside, she turned the knob, expecting to just go out that way, but it, too, refused to budge.

"It's a double locking door—from the outside and inside. There's no key."

Savannah crossed her arms and faced Logan. "Clearly."

"Do you have your cell? Just call Jack or Leigh."

She turned away from him, her eyes wide as she peered around the dark basement. With just the single light, it looked like something out of a horror movie. Why hadn't her mama added more lighting down here? That was going on her list right after the damn doorknob. "It's sitting on the front desk."

"You left your cell phone unattended? Someone could take it."

A sarcastic laugh burst from her lips. "Really, who? The only person staying here is you!"

"Point taken." He pulled his own phone from his pocket and glanced at Savannah, those green eyes of his drawing her in. "I'll call. What's the number?" At her puzzled expression, he dropped his arm to his side. "You don't know their numbers?"

"They're in my cell phone. No one knows anyone's phone number by heart anymore."

"I do."

"Yeah, but you're weird with numbers. Always have been."

He grinned and she knew he was thinking of the time she'd asked him to tutor her in math. It'd taken fifteen minutes of stalling and annoyed grunts for her to actually say the word *help*. And then it'd taken all her effort not to deck him when he said, "Sure, but you'll have to say please."

"Why do you always do that?" Savannah asked, annoyed.

He looked around. "What?"

"Smirk all the time. Like you know something I don't know, and you're refusing to tell me."

At that, the smirk returned, and Savannah contemplated the decking him idea again. "Now you're just doing it to piss me off."

Logan shook his head. "I assure you, I never deliberately try to piss you off. Though it somehow happens all the same. Anyway, it's fine. I'll just call Travis."

"*No*. You can't call anyone in town. I'll be the laughing stock—a week on the job and I get myself locked in the basement. Don't call them. We'll just have to wait for Jack and Leigh to return."

"Where did they go?"

Savannah walked over and sat down on a broken wooden bench. It used to sit on the front porch. She did her homework on it when she was little. "Sal's."

"Well, that settles it." Logan released a long breath and

motioned for her to move over so he could sit beside her. "Might as well get comfortable. We'll be here for a while."

"This is my seat. Find your own." Her body might react in crazy ways to him, but that didn't mean she had to give it any extra opportunities. Savannah crossed her arms and kept her focus away from him. So she didn't see him lean in close and wasn't at all prepared to be picked up, his strong arms cradling her close, his woodsy scent intoxicating her senses. A sigh broke free before she could contain it, and he laughed just before setting her back down on the other side of the bench.

"What exactly do you think you're doing?"

"What does it look like? Moving you over."

Fury raged through her, but another part of her was more than a little curious at how easily he'd lifted her. She wondered if he worked out, if he lifted weights…if he lifted women before placing them in his bed. Did he hover over them, his eyes on theirs before kissing them?

Suddenly, the cold basement felt very, very hot.

Clearing her throat, she crossed her arms and then her legs, frustrated at the sudden burning sensation radiating from the center of her back and how very close it felt to jealousy. She had no claim on Logan, but that didn't keep her from hating the idea of some other woman claiming him as hers. But that was stupid. Logan had never once been Savannah's.

She thought of the long summer days they'd shared together, laying out below the clouds and the stars, nothing to keep them company but their thoughts and each other. It was then she realized what a great voice Logan had. Deep but smooth. There was nothing scratchy or rough about it.

His voice walked the line between speech and song, and she could listen to him talk all day without growing tired. She'd wondered why she never noticed it before, but then realized Will had always been there, too.

Will.

The single thing both linking and separating them. After Will's death, she'd hoped Logan would become a close friend, someone she could talk to who understood. But soon, her attraction to him became too much. She found herself brushing her hair before their visits, checking her breath, smoothing her clothes. It was foolish, and though she'd felt shame the entire walk over, her insides would light up the moment she saw him. Young Logan was all worn cargo shorts and white T-shirts, his golden skin tanned from their hours in the sun, his hair almost white in places, wheat or honey in others. It was impossible to look at him without staring.

But he never tried to impress her, never hinted that he felt anything significant for her other than as his dead best friend's girl. Until one day while they were cloud watching, she allowed him to catch her staring. Their gazes held as his hand glided over the blanket, and then her breath caught as his fingers ran over her open palm before closing around her hand. It was nothing and everything. They didn't speak for three days after.

But then the worst storm Maple had ever seen rolled in and she'd had to see him, had to know that they were still okay, that he was still her friend. Only, when she found him, nothing about the look in his eyes said friendship…and in the next moment, everything had changed. But why? Why did anything have to change?

Why did he have to leave?

The thought made her heart ache all over again, and finally, unable to sit still another second, Savannah jumped up. She couldn't sit this close to the man without at least asking him the one question that had poisoned her mind with doubt for so many years.

"Why did you do it?"

Logan looked up at her like she'd lost her mind, and maybe she had. The stress of losing her mother, coupled with the bed-and-breakfast's financial woes, were enough to do her in. And then the one person who could shake her insides with one look came strutting into town, demanding to sleep in the room across from hers. How could any woman of a right mind stay sane?

He eyed the bench, then her. "I wanted to sit down."

"Not that." She took a step back and wrapped her arms around her stomach, needing to support herself if she hoped to say her next words. "Why did you kiss me...and then leave?"

Logan snapped his mouth closed, his eyes on the woman in front of him, the one question he'd hoped she'd never ask sucking the oxygen from his lungs. Still, he refused to look away from her.

"I..."

The memory came back to him as though it'd happened moments before. The storm had blown in, rain beating down outside, drowning out everything. He and Savannah had met every day for two weeks, and for two weeks those visits were the only thing keeping him going. Will's death had thrown him in a way he never thought possible. He doubted everything, but most of all he doubted his own humanity. How could he be alive when a person like Will wasn't?

And then he'd changed everything by holding her hand.

He'd been itching to get out of the house, to go over to Savannah's and tell her something, anything to make her talk to him again. He wanted to admit the thing that ate at his insides everyday, that both made him and destroyed him every time he saw her.

That he loved her.

Loved her with a sort of depth that would never end, that would only grow and tangle and bloom. That it wasn't two weeks worth of time with her. It was years upon years, knowing he didn't deserve her, but not caring. Especially not in that moment.

Will was gone, and he wanted to ache. He wanted to rip off the Band-Aid and pour acid on it, and then do it all over again, until he could no longer stand the pain. And then his drunken-ass father had stormed into his room, shouting all the things Logan already knew—that he'd be deployed in two days, and with any luck, he'd find the same fate as Will.

Angry, he'd pushed out the back door, allowing the pouring rain to drench his clothes and heart, mixing with tears he could no longer hold back. How he ended up at their spot, he didn't know. He'd never walked there before, but that day he wasn't thinking, only acting. And that's when she found him, wrecked and nearly sobbing. It was like she saw straight into his soul, and in two steps they were together, arms wild and frantic, their lips finally saying all the things they couldn't say out loud. Then, what began as a reckless kiss turned into more as his hands explored her body, reaching for her shirt as she reached for his. They were moments from succumbing to each other right there in front of God and whoever else might be watching.

But then the rain slowed, and with the clear sky came clearer thinking. He'd made a terrible mistake. She'd been right to feel regret the other day, but he now he saw only hope. How had he not seen it before? She wanted him to fill Will's spot, and he never could. Not in a lifetime of trying. But how could he explain that to her? He knew the guilt would come for her, too, and he didn't want her to suffer the way he did. He cared for her too much for that. So he left.

How could he help her see that he'd done her a favor? His only thought had been to save her from more pain.

"Was it me?" she asked, bringing him back to the moment.

Ah hell…

He shook his head and stood, unable to speak. It took every bit of effort to keep his eyes on hers, to take in the pain there. He'd never noticed it behind the anger and sass, or realized that after all these years, the problem wasn't that he'd left, but that he'd hurt her. He thought she'd get over it, move on, and remember him as the asshole who'd kissed her one rain-drenched summer day. But he could see it had meant more to her than he'd ever guessed. The realization made him want to pull her into his arms and never let her go, to protect her from ever being hurt again. But that wasn't his story with Savannah. It was Will's.

Forcing himself to draw a breath, he swallowed and took a step toward her. "No, it wasn't you."

"Then what? I thought…I don't know. That we were…"

"We were."

"Then, why—"

Finally his last bit of control snapped and he started for her. "Because my best friend was killed in action, and I came home and did what? Serve his memory? Volunteer at some damn charity, or vow to follow the straight and narrow? No, I kiss the one person he loved most in the world. And not just kissed. I wanted you. I wanted you like I had never wanted anything, and when I finally touched you, felt your skin against mine, I couldn't back away. I tried. God above, I tried. But then you were there, and my mind was shit, and all I wanted was to make everything worse. So I did. I walked myself straight to hell's gate, and I have never been more sorry for anything in my life."

That was a lie. Logan wasn't sorry for the kiss. He was too selfish to be sorry for it. But he *was* sorry he'd hurt her.

Silence found them, their eyes still locked as each of their hearts pounded in each of their chests.

"God, say something," Logan said, desperate for her to relieve the silence—the throbbing in his head and heart.

Then the door to the basement opened and Jack stood there, staring between them. "Everything okay? I heard shouting."

"Yeah, just coming back up," Savannah said slowly. She turned away, following after her brother, but she stopped at the door, her hand tapping against the wood. It was then that Logan realized she was shaking.

"There's a difference between guilt and regret. And I don't regret it. Maybe I should, but I don't. I'm *not* sorry. I wasn't then, and I'm not now." She propped the door open with a loose brick from the floor and then disappeared up the stairs, leaving Logan alone once more.

Chapter Nine

Savannah woke at four-thirty the next morning to a wail that cut straight through her skull, refusing to be ignored. Jumping up, she grabbed the bat she kept beside her bed and rubbed her eyes, poised to hit someone or something if it came into her room. That was, if she could keep from falling over.

She'd spent all night tossing and turning, replaying Logan's words. A part of her wanted to go to him and hug him close, tell him that she understood. The guilt had a way of hanging around, showing up at the worst moments, reminding her that she might not regret kissing Logan, but she'd burn all the same. He was Will's best friend. Will, who had died mere weeks before that kiss. Thinking through it in that way always cemented her guilt. Still, if it was a mistake, it was their mistake, not just his. They both loved Will, but that didn't mean they should forever live their lives in memory of him. But knowing the right way to feel and actually feeling that way were not the same things.

The wailing continued, and Savannah forced her brain to focus enough to pinpoint the source of the noise. A smoke alarm.

No, no, no! You are not burning down on me, bed-and-breakfast. I haven't fixed you yet!

Tossing open her door, she started out into the hall, prepared to tell the fire it could go to hell, but there was no smoke. No raging flames. No signs at all that the bed-and-breakfast was indeed on fire. *Hmm.*

Easing down the stairs, she found the smoke alarm in the common room blaring like a baby who couldn't reach his pacifier. Searching the room, she grabbed a chair and placed it under the alarm, then stood on it to press the reset button, feeling pretty darn pleased with herself, until nothing happened. She pressed it again, held it down, counted to five, then did it all over again, but the freaking thing refused to stop.

"Ugh! Shut up!"

"When you're done screaming at it, can you turn it off?"

Savannah spun to see Logan a few feet away from her, his hair sticking out in random directions, a lazy grin on his face. Her gaze drifted from his hair down to his bare chest, over the simple black cross tattooed on his left pectoral muscle, to his low-hanging flannel pajama pants and how *very* clear it was that he wore nothing else beneath them. She swallowed, suddenly not at all concerned with the alarm or its refusal to do what she asked.

"Anna? The alarm?"

"What? Oh—right. I can't turn it off. It won't listen to me."

A smile played at his lips as he neared. "Maybe that's because you're wearing a Mickey Mouse T-shirt." He leaned in closer and thumbed the hem of her nightshirt, his fingertips grazing her thigh. And holy shitake mushroom. Warmth spread from that tiny point of contact, up her leg, settling in her stomach, her breathing suddenly very uneven. "And no pants. To be honest, I'm having a hard time focusing, too."

"Funny," she said, attempting to control her voice—and her out-of-control heart—but a blush crept across her cheeks all the same. She'd been so eager to get the wailing to end, she didn't stop to think about what—or how little—she wore. Her eyes dropped to her bare legs, the T-shirt barely covering her lower goocs. So *not* the kind of thing she should be sporting around Logan, especially with all the extra tingles and inappropriate thoughts running around in her brain.

"Hit the reset button."

Savannah placed her hands on her hips, which caused the shirt to hitch up. Logan's gaze dropped. "Right, because I'm a complete idiot and didn't think to hit the reset. Try again."

The grin spread. "All right. Then how about this." He swept her into his arms, one hand dangerously close to her breast, the other griping her thighs, her body pressed firmly against his rock-hard pectoral muscles. Forget the alarm. Forget the B and B. Forget everything. She'd just as soon stay right there, cradled in his strong arms. Her already heated insides burst into flames, desire tempting logic, until it was all she could do not to lean toward him—see if he'd take the prompt and kiss her.

Instead, he set her down beside the chair and took her

place. He hit the reset, which did nothing at all, so *ha!* Then without another thought, he slid open the battery compartment, popped out the battery, and tossed it to Savannah. The wailing ceased. "Done. Anything else?" Stepping down from the chair, he stood a foot and a half, at most, away from her. A soapy, woodsy, too-sexy-for-anything-good-to-come-of-it smell hit her nose, and she wondered if he showered at night or in the morning. Or did he do both? Suddenly, she pictured him in the shower, soapy and—

Pull yourself together, woman.

Her eyes lifted to find Logan watching her, his hair as messy as ever. She ached to run her hands through the tangled locks, to smooth them back into place, then allow her hands to slip down his back and...

"Savannah?"

"What? Oh. No, that's all." Flustered, she turned away from him, thoughts of their basement encounter still fresh in her mind. Was it possible that Logan still felt more for her than he let on? Maybe he had then, but now? Surely not, but then why did he get so worked up when he talked about the kiss? Why did it sound like he'd regretted more about that day than just their betrayal of Will?

"Okay. See you in the morning."

"Thanks. Good night." She placed the battery on the front desk and started for the kitchen, but the sound of her name had her looking up. "Hm?"

"You aren't going back to sleep?"

"I wasn't sleeping so well to begin with. Thought I'd make some coffee."

He bit his lip and stared at her. Could he sense why she hadn't slept? Did he have the same struggle? She studied his features, trying to find something deeper within them, but he wasn't giving anything away.

"Care for company?"

"If you stay, I'll have to go put on clothes."

"How about we both agree to not stare at how little the other is wearing?"

"Impossible. Look at you," she said as she continued on into the kitchen. "But join me if you like. You're my only paying customer. Might as well keep you happy."

He walked close behind her, warmth radiating off him, and Savannah thought of what it would be like to be pulled into those defined arms of his, pressed up against the wall, all thought gone but the passion between them. But maybe that passion was just in her. He'd made it very clear he was sorry they'd kissed in the first place, and though a part of her was angry at him, for that and the way he left her all those years ago, she understood. How could she not?

"Sit," he ordered, as he pulled two mugs down from the cabinet and began making coffee. "Cream no sugar?"

"How did you know?"

"I pay attention."

Her heart throbbed and she pushed away a smile. She wondered what would have happened between them if he hadn't left. Would they have been able to put Will behind them and be happy? Of course, that assumed he wanted her at all, and clearly he didn't, right? He'd left.

Logan went to work making her coffee, then poured a black cup for himself and sat beside her on one of the barstools. She wanted to ask why he'd left and what happened after. She knew he'd enlisted for five years, so he couldn't have stayed either way. Still, she wondered what would have happened if they'd said good-bye. Would they have written each other? Would he have come back to see her? Would he eventually have felt for her what she felt for him? Those weren't easy questions and their answers would likely cause her more pain, so she settled on something easier.

"Do you like real estate?"

He stopped mid way to sipping his coffee and cocked a brow at her. "What?"

"Aren't you in real estate?"

"Ah, that." He set down the cup, holding it between both hands, seemingly deep in thought. "It's not what I would have done."

"What do you mean? You chose the job right?"

"In a way."

Savannah watched his face, searching his expression for what he might mean, but again, he revealed nothing. "Did you get your degree?"

"I did. Double major in management and economics."

She smiled. "Always in love with numbers."

"They come easy to me," he said with a shrug.

"So if you wouldn't have picked real estate, then why did you go into that field?"

He stared out into the kitchen. "Want some eggs?" Slipping from the stool, he went to the fridge and pulled out a carton of eggs, and then bread and butter to make toast.

"Are you refusing to answer my question, Logan Park?"

He leveled his gaze on hers. "Yes."

"Why?"

"Add that to the refuse to answer list."

"That's hardly fair."

He laughed. "I never claimed to be fair."

Huffing, Savannah went around the island and reached across him for the bread. Her arm gently grazed his bare skin, sending a jolt through her that nearly caused her to drop the slice. Her eyes lifted to see if he'd felt it, too, but he was focused on her arm, still brushing his stomach, and his breathing was uneven.

"I'm sorry." The words were barely a whisper, but as their eyes locked, she knew she wasn't sorry at all. She wanted to be near him, wanted to see his face change when they touched. It awoke her heart in the best and worst ways. They shouldn't be doing this. Then or now. So, why couldn't she stop? Why couldn't she just be good?

The people of Maple respected the Hale name, and here she was risking her family's reputation, over and over again, subjecting herself to more gossip. All for a man who'd never once said he cared for her at all. Who hadn't even liked her until Will's death.

Stepping away so she could think more clearly, she popped the bread into the toaster and turned to him, crossing her arms. His gaze went immediately to her legs and she followed his stare down to see her shirt had ridden up, exposing the bottoms of her black panties. Her face lit with heat as she tugged the shirt back into place, and Logan became very focused on the eggs. She couldn't be sure if he cared for her, but his body definitely reacted around her. Still, wanting wasn't the same as caring.

Desperate to ease the tension, she went back to their conversation. She would try the friend thing—or at least not enemies. "So if not real estate, then what did you want to do?"

"I don't know."

Savannah watched in awe as he folded the eggs over and over, scrambling them into fluffy perfection. She'd never been able to cook eggs without scorching them, but Logan made it seem easy. He made a lot of things seem easy.

"I used to say I wanted to own my own business," he said. "That was the logic behind the management major. I thought it'd help me learn the basics."

"And what about economics?"

He went still again, lifted his gaze to the wall, then shrugged and went back to work on the eggs. "Just something I needed to add on."

Savannah sensed a deeper story there, but she had too many questions to focus on silly stuff like majors. "Did you want to move back here after you left the army?"

A sarcastic laugh slipped from his lips. "With my dad around? No thanks."

Savannah tried not to feel the burn of his words. She wanted to tell him that his father wasn't the only one in Maple that might want him home, that plenty of people cared about him, but she'd left, too. How could she argue with him wanting to get away from a man like his father when she'd left two amazing parents behind?

"Right. Logan…"

"I'm trying," he said. "But it's hard to answer questions about what brought me to this point in my life. I second guess things all the time, or wish I'd made different decisions." His deep green eyes held hers. "I feel regrets that I wonder if I'll ever overcome. But this is where I am now, and there's nothing that can change that. Some things can't be undone — or *re*done. Can they?"

She stared at him. Was he asking what she thought he

was asking?

But before she could answer, the sound of someone walking into the kitchen made them both glance over. "Who's cooking?" Jack asked, taking a seat on one of barstools. Then he eyed each of them. "Why are you both half naked?"

Savannah fumbled with the toast, burning her fingertips as she dropped the slice onto a plate, which Jack immediately grabbed. He took a giant bite of toast before placing it back down.

"Hey! I took a hit for that one," she said, sucking her singed thumb, refusing to look at Logan, though she could feel his gaze on her. "Didn't you hear the smoke alarm this morning?"

"Nah. I sleep like a baby." Jack stole the toast again and took another bite, earning a death glare from his sister.

"Where's Leigh?" she asked, grabbing the now-cooled toast before he could scarf down the rest.

Jack looked at her. "Do I have 'Leigh's assistant' tattooed on my forehead? I don't know. Call her. She's probably in town again. I don't know why you keep sending her to the hardware store. She has no clue what she's doing."

Savannah opened her mouth to say that she hadn't sent Leigh anywhere, but closed it. Leigh had been spending a lot of time at Jim's Hardware lately, and the blonde triplets had said Jim was secretly dating someone in town. Maybe… No, Jack would kill Jim if he went after Leigh. Best friends didn't go after little sisters. Did they? But Jack wouldn't be here much longer, so…

"Hey, when do you have to be back?" she asked him. If Leigh was dating Jim then maybe she'd admit it to Savannah once Jack left town.

"Back where?"

"It's late spring. Shouldn't you be playing?"

Jack looked away, and Savannah watched him take a fresh slice of toast from her plate, throw on some of the eggs Logan had placed beside the toast, and fold it all up into a makeshift sandwich. "I'm on bereavement leave for two weeks."

"And it's been nearly two weeks."

He shrugged.

"What's going on?"

"Nothing. Leave it."

"Jack?"

"I'm heading to the shower. We're supposed to be at the town meeting at ten."

Ah, the town meeting. They were supposed to be only once a month, but with the spring festival coming up, an extra meeting had been added. Or so they said. Savannah still thought this was all just a way to ask her in public, with witnesses, what the Hales planned to do with the B and B.

Jack stood up to leave, and Savannah reached out to stop him, eager to ask more questions about why he was here instead of playing, when Logan shook his head slightly.

What was going on?

Tucking away her concern, she dug into what was left of her eggs—*sans* toast, thanks to her brother—curious if the bed-and-breakfast had always been this full of secrets.

With Jane Hale running it, likely not.

Logan set out down the sidewalk on Main Street, his eyes covered by his shades so no one could see him taking stock of his old town. He passed Maple's Bakery and thought of the baseball team raiding it after a local win, of the cupcakes handed out for all the players, and of Will giving his to Savannah instead.

What would his friend say if he could see him now— hanging all over Savannah, desperate for any bit of attention she would throw at him. Would Will support his friend or would he hate him? Logan tried to think how he would feel if the situation were reversed and thought he'd want Savannah to be happy. But happy with his best friend? Maybe. Maybe not…

"Logan?"

He turned to find Mrs. Cooke walking out of the bakery, her face etched with worry. "Are you okay, honey?"

He shook himself from his thoughts before they ruined his mood. "Um, yes ma'am. Is there something I can do for you?"

She walked toward him. "You know, forgive me for saying this, but I always thought you and Savannah would make a fine pair. Your personalities are so alike."

Logan laughed. "You mean we're both stubborn."

Mrs. Cooke laughed as well. "Perhaps. She's a sweet girl, my Savannah. I'd sure like to see her with a good man. I think Will wanted that for her, too."

"What do you mean?"

"Ah, it was just something he said before you boys left for Afghanistan. He'd come into the kitchen at the B and B to pick up some food his mama had ordered, and I asked— probably like everybody else in town—if he planned to propose to Savannah before he left. He looked out the back window and said, 'No. Savannah should marry the guy who has her heart. That ain't me.' I thought he was just feeling off because he was leaving, but now I wonder if maybe he saw something before the rest of us."

Logan's mouth went slack, his mind churning. He thought of Will finding the photo Logan kept of Savannah, the argument they'd gotten into, and the words he said — *I thought it was just her.* Was it possible Savannah had feelings for him even before Will died, and Will knew?

A dozen moments flashed through his mind — small comments from Savannah in high school, and the time she got stranded on the boat. She could have put the battery in herself — she definitely knew how — but she asked Logan to do it, to stay and ride back with her just to be safe. Had that all been to spend time with him?

Maybe he wasn't merely a replacement for Will after all. Maybe Will had been the replacement for him.

"Care to help an old lady to the meeting?" Mrs. Cooke took his arm and started toward the courthouse, making Logan unable to do anything but follow along. They walked up the side steps, where the wooden door was propped open so anyone interested could come in to listen.

Mrs. Cooke patted Logan's cheek as she stepped away from him.

"Thank you, dear. You were always a nice boy. It's a wonderful thing to see you become such a good man. And something tells me I'm not the only one to notice how good you are. How good you've always been." She nodded to the second to last row of chairs, where Savannah sat beside Leigh, and Logan's stomach clenched tight.

"Right."

Logan's phone vibrated inside his pocket, saving him from the conversation, and giving him an opportunity to step out so he could think. He pulled his cell out and motioned to the door. "Sorry, I need to take this."

"Of course, dear."

"Park," Logan said, once he was outside.

"Logan? It's Chloe."

He grinned. "I think we've been over this."

"Right, right. So, listen. I have a problem. I was trying to add your signature to the Jekyll Island property contract, but it keeps saying I don't have authorization to edit the document. Do you know the password? Why is it protected anyway? Are you planning to fire me and haven't told me yet, because if you are then—"

Logan sighed heavily. "I'm not firing you. I have no idea why it's protected, but if you could put the file on the server, I can e-sign it tonight and resave it for you. Then just print the document and mail it tomorrow."

"Oh my God, so you're not firing me? That's what my boyfriend said when I called him, but then this file thing happened, and I thought—"

Logan watched through the open door as Mayor Kitchings hobbled to the front of the room, gavel in hand to start the meeting. His gray hair was combed over his bald spot, and like always, he wore khaki pants and a plaid button down. It could be the middle of a heat wave, Logan thought, and the mayor would be in his plaid.

"I'm sorry, Chloe. Can I call you back?"

"Oh! Sorry, I know you're busy. Sure. I'll put the file on the server."

"Thank you. Just print and mail it tomorrow. Okay?"

"Will do. And Logan?"

"Yes?"

"Thanks for not firing me."

Logan laughed. "Anytime."

He slipped back inside just as Mayor Kitchings hit the gavel against the podium, signaling for everyone to quiet down. Folding chairs sat in straight lines, five by ten, then a wide aisle, and another section of five by ten. Logan doubted a hundred people from the town would show, but then he'd been surprised before.

He took his seat in the row behind Savannah and leaned back in his chair, fighting the urge to ask her if they could talk, to find out if what Mrs. Cooke suggested was true. But the truth was, he wasn't ready to ask her. He had to see if she still had feelings for him. Otherwise, he'd dredge up all these old emotions for nothing. But how could he find out without asking her outright?

Others from town filtered in, and Logan tried to put this new revelation out of his mind, at least until he figured out what to do. It was the first time Logan had ever sat in on a town hall meeting, but with his firm taking over the bed-and-breakfast soon, he felt it necessary to learn how they worked. And Logan knew the mayor would ask the Hales about the B and B, and he wanted to hear what Savannah would say. She'd yet to officially take it over, and he wondered about her plans for it. A part of him knew he should convince her to leave, to sell it. It was better for the firm, but the truth was he didn't want to see her go.

"First things first, we need to confirm station directors for Maple's spring fair next week. I believe we've created a tentative list." He motioned to Martha Long, his long time administrative assistant, who passed him a sheet of paper. "Ah, here we go. There will be ten stations, each run by a business owner. Any objections?" When no one argued, he continued. "Savannah Hale?"

Savannah's head snapped up from where she sat in the row ahead of Logan's. "Yes?"

"We have you covering for the bed-and-breakfast. Is that fine with you?"

"Of course."

"Good, then," he said, his gray brows knitting together as he read the list. "You will cover the kissing booth. The station will be at the end of Main Street, right before you reach the bed-and-breakfast. Martha will email you the details and—"

Savannah jumped up. "Wait. Sorry, Mayor Kitchings, but what did you say I was covering?"

"The kissing booth," Logan answered for the mayor, having a little too much fun with this fact. He fought the urge to laugh, sure that if he did, Savannah would have all his things out on the front porch of the bed-and-breakfast before he made it back there.

"I heard him," she hissed at Logan. "What I'm asking is what does that involve exactly? And why can't I handle face painting or bobbing for apples?"

The mayor appeared genuinely perplexed. "Claire Mae is handling face painting. Jim already signed up for apples."

"Signed up? I never—"

"Actually," Leigh interrupted. " You were busy in the attic, so I took it upon myself to sign up for you when Martha came by earlier in the week. I thought the kissing booth would be cute, plus..." She leaned into Savannah and attempted a whisper, but in the quiet room she might as well have shouted. "I thought you could use a little action. Test out some potential dates without anyone the wiser." Leigh looked pleased with herself, until Savannah turned slowly toward her sister like a monster ready to bite off its victim's head. Leigh's smile dropped away. "Or maybe not. But don't be mad. It's probably just little kids anyway."

"Is it only kids, Mayor?" Travis Axon asked from the back of the room. Everyone turned to look at the young sheriff like it was the most sensible question in the world. Travis's dark, curly hair looked as out of control as ever as he waited for the mayor's answer.

Mayor Kitchings looked to Martha, who whispered in his ear, and then he addressed the crowd again. "Any paying customer."

Travis's eyes switched to Savannah, a smile spreading across his face, and Logan burst out laughing, unable to hold it in another second.

"This should be interesting," Logan said. "Can I pay to watch, Mayor?"

He consulted Martha again, just as Savannah spun around, her hands on her hips in anger.

"We see no reason why not," the mayor said. "Now, to continue on with the list."

"Wait, I didn't agree to this," Savannah said. "I..."

Logan leaned forward, draping his arm over the back of her chair. "Now come on, Anna, surely you aren't going to disappoint the townspeople."

Her eyes searched those around her, and Logan's smile widened. He would pay very good money to watch this disaster.

"No, I don't want to disappoint anyone. I'll do it." Savannah sat back down and crossed her arms, her mouth set, but he could tell she was trying to find a way out without offending half the town. Only that was the thing about Maple. Once the town set its mind to something, you either went along with it or suffered exile. She had no choice.

They listened to the mayor rattle off the rest of the list then move through town business. All the while an idea started through Logan's mind. Suddenly, he thought Savannah at the kissing booth wasn't such a bad idea.

Not a bad idea at all.

Chapter Ten

Savannah peered down at the outfit Leigh had set out for her, a note on top telling her to be open minded. Open minded her ass. This was just ridiculous. Almost as ridiculous as that town meeting yesterday. Thankfully, they ran out of time before she had to answer questions about the B and B. Even now, she wasn't 100 percent sure what she would say.

One thing at a time. And presently, she had a kissing both to get to.

With a long sigh, she went to her chest of drawers and pulled out a tank top and chambray shorts, then laid them beside the outfit Leigh had chosen. Her sister's pick was navy and red tiny plaid shorts and a sleeveless white polo— the kind of outfit those golfer girls who drove around selling drinks to men three times their age wore. She wasn't wearing it. No way, no how. She didn't even want to *do* this.

A knock had her tucking her towel tighter around her as she opened the door, expecting to find Leigh staring back at her, but instead it was Logan.

"I thought you were Leigh." She fidgeted with her towel. The last thing she needed was for the thing to drop to the ground and him to see her female parts before she'd offered them for his viewing pleasure. Which then made her wonder if she wanted to offer them for his viewing pleasure. No, not at all. She didn't want Logan seeing her parts, and she certainly didn't want to see his parts, and—

Oh my God. *Parts?* What was she, eight years old? Clearly, she needed to get out more. She'd just decided to ask Logan what he needed, so he could leave her to ponder this, when she noticed him staring.

Logan's eyes drifted over her shoulders, likely still sprinkled with water droplets, and then slowly down her towel, causing goose bumps to burst across her skin. She loved the feel of his eyes on her, how it was as though he couldn't help himself, like he found her too beautiful to look away. The thought made her far giddier than it should.

Clearing his throat, he raised his gaze to her face, one eye slightly squinted. "You're trying to kill me, aren't you?"

"What?"

"Nothing. Leigh said you have to be at the booth in fifteen minutes."

Savannah exhaled. "All right." She's just turned back to her outfit problem when Logan added, "Wear the tank. It's you. And you should never be anyone other than you."

She smiled at him, the goose bumps returning for entirely different reasons. "Thanks."

"Anytime." He tapped his cell against his palm. "All right, then. See you down there."

"Wait... You're going?"

"Wouldn't miss it." He winked at her and then closed the door.

Fantastic.

Deciding it was best to just get it over with, she threw on her clothes and went to work on her hair and makeup.

One day of kissing. How bad could it be?

She took one final look at herself, grabbed her cell, and headed outside.

The weather had kept its promise. There was a bright blue sky above with cotton ball clouds shielding the sun from time to time. The day reminded Savannah of her childhood and made her miss her parents so badly that she nearly went back to the bed-and-breakfast to wallow in memories. But she'd known most of these people her whole life. The town was like an extended family, and she didn't want to let her family down.

Mayor Kitchings had broadcasted the event on a few major radio stations in Atlanta, and his reach had proven wise. Main Street grew more and more crowded by the minute, with kids walking hand in hand with their parents, and strollers for those too young to walk.

Savannah glanced down at her chosen outfit. She'd gone with the plaid shorts, but paired them with a basic white tank top, blending the two looks. Her strawberry blond hair hung in waves down her back, and she'd put on a full face of makeup, including an extra swipe of vanilla-flavored gloss for good measure. Let the kissing begin.

"We have a little problem," Leigh said, catching Savannah as she started for the booth. Like always, Leigh wore dark colors—in this case, a charcoal tank top and black shorts. A bright blue headband held back her hair.

"What is it?" Savannah asked.

"Um, that." Leigh pointed to the booth, and Savannah stopped mid-step.

"What the hell is *that*?"

There was a line. A very long line. And of that line, very few were kids. Savannah had pictured herself kissing young boys on the cheek, them embarrassed and her patting their cute little heads, the whole thing very innocent and sweet. But there was nothing sweet about this line, unless you counted Frank, who in all likelihood just waited there to tell Savannah hello.

No, this line was comprised of teen boys, college boys, men her age, older men—all who had no business waiting in a line to kiss a twenty-something woman. She reminded herself that this was for charity, like those date auctions where hot guys took the stage, and women bid on dates. Only, that would be better than this. A thousand, million times better than this.

Could she kiss them all on the cheek? Surely she didn't have to kiss them on the lips, right? What if one became squirrely and tried to use his tongue and—

"I'm going to kill you for getting me into this."

Leigh cringed beside her. "Apparently the flyer has a photo of you. In a bikini."

"What? Where would they get that?" Savannah screamed, rushing up to the stop sign at the end of the drive, where a bright pink flyer had been taped up. Sure enough, on the back was a giant photo of her in a bikini and beside it were the words: $2 PER KISS.

"Jesus C."

"I know. Only two dollars. Shouldn't it be more like

five?"

Savannah glared at her sister. "The town is whoring me out, and you're worried over the amount?"

"Right. I'm sorry. But just remember, it's for a good cause."

"*This* is for a good cause?" Savannah motioned to her bikinied self.

Leigh made a face and shrugged slowly before turning her attention to the line. "Well, you better get started. I just hope they weren't expecting you to be in the bikini. Because, awkward."

Savannah closed her eyes. *Mama, if you're there, I'd appreciate a little fixing here. Or at least some heavy alcohol.*

The booth was a wooden table covered in a pink table-cloth, with a floral arrangement on top and a banner tied to the front. Savannah didn't have the courage to look at the banner for fear she'd see a larger version of the flyer. Reminding herself that this was all to help the town, she took her seat and smiled at the first person—or rather boy—in line. He couldn't be more than eight, a smattering of freckles across his face, and Savannah released a slow breath.

"Hi, there."

"I have two dollars," he said, passing her the two bills. Savannah smiled and kissed his cheek and he ran off to a group of friends nearby. She released another breath. Maybe she could do this after all.

But then her smile dropped away as she saw the next person in line—a man who had to be fifty or older, with a very obvious gold wedding band on his left hand. "Um…"

"Two dollars, right? Well, I have four. Does that mean I get two kisses?" He waggled his eyebrows and leaned in, a rush of smoky breath hitting her face and *Oh my God!* She started to close her eyes, prepared to suffer in the name of charity, but before Mr. Marlboro could kiss her, Logan cut in front of him.

"Hey!" the man protested. "I waited an hour for this kiss."

Logan shrugged. "Sorry, man, I have a special pass for today. Like at Disney World, where you get to skip the line. So I'd like to take my turn now." He turned back to face Savannah, a giant smile on his face and a giant wad of bills in his left hand.

"What are you doing?" Savannah whispered.

"What does it look like? Saving your *pretty ass*," he whispered back.

"Well, hurry up," the man grumbled.

"You can't save me from this insanity," Savannah said. "Not sure even God himself could save me from this line."

Logan's gaze shifted to the crowd, then returned to her. "We'll see." He leaned in closer, ready for their kiss.

"You can't do this," she whispered, but she couldn't keep her eyes from dropping to his lips. Did they feel the way she remembered? Did he still taste like mint and summer rain? Did she want to kiss him? No. Absolutely not.

Yes.

He counted out two dollars and placed them in the change box. "I can. Now kiss me." He tilted her chin up, his gaze flicking to her lips before returning to her eyes. "Stop me now if you're going to." A moment passed, her chance to tell him no, to push him away, but with her eyes locked on his—the green shimmering bright in the sun, a hint of challenge behind them—all she could do was breathe in answer.

As he closed the distance slowly, his breath hit her mouth, warm and inviting, and then his lips pressed softly to hers, sampling the feel of them. Goose bumps rose across her skin, and it took every bit of control in her not to moan in satisfaction, her insides screaming out *finally*! And then just as she'd decided to deepen the kiss, he pulled away, his eyes closed for a moment, then opening, full of confusion.

"Anna?"

She couldn't respond as her own eyes found the table. Any response at all would have her confessing everything, how much she missed him, all the sleepless nights wondering where he was, the constant ache in her chest that lifted every time she saw him now.

"Anna, look at me."

"I can't."

"Look at me."

Her gaze lifted, and she knew she was showing too much emotion, but she couldn't help it. In that single kiss she'd felt more relief than she thought possible. Like finally, finally, she could breathe.

"Again," Logan said.

"What? No, the line —"

Logan counted out two more dollars and placed them in the box.

"Hey, you had your turn," the man behind him argued, with several others chiming in with the same. But Savannah could barely hear them, could barely hear anything beyond the pounding of her pulse in her ears.

"Again," Logan repeated, slowly this time.

Savannah's bottom lip trembled, all their history — the hurt she'd felt, the longing that remained even after the pain subsided—bubbling up. "Logan…"

This time he didn't wait for a reply. He rushed in, his lips connecting with hers, his fingers threading into her hair. And then she was standing, the need to be close to him too great to keep her still another moment. Her lips parted, and his tongue slid over her teeth and her tongue, tasting and feeling, and Savannah lost all control. She moaned against his lips—until Leigh cleared her throat loudly.

"Oh!" Savannah pulled away this time, her cheeks burning as she caught the crowd watching them. The mayor. Mrs. Cooke. The blonde triplets.

Oh my God.

Everyone was going to talk. They all knew now. There was no hiding this. She pressed her fingertips to her tingly lips. Though the kiss had lasted all of three seconds, Savannah felt breathless. Her heart and mind were at odds, one telling her to stop this from going any further, to save her name, the other saying to forget all her worries and live for once.

"One, two," Logan said, counting out more dollars, which did little more than anger the people behind him. Several walked away, calling out the unfairness of it, but Logan never let his resolve waver.

Logan dropped the bills into the change box then met her eyes again. With a single exhale, he leaned in and Savannah knew she couldn't push him away. Not when they were nineteen, and not now. His lips grazed hers, first soft, then a touch harder, his body closer, his mouth moving over hers, drawing her in. His fingertips slipped through her hair, cradling her head as he deepened the kiss, his mouth taking ownership. He kissed her like there was no one around, like nothing else in the world mattered, and she found herself falling into it, ready to go wherever he took her. Her heart raced away in her chest, and she feared it might never settle down, that she might never recover... And there was still a long line stretching from her booth, a dozen or more kisses still to come if he planned to wait them all out. How would she ever get away from this day with her heart intact?

With obvious effort he pulled away, his eyes so dark they were nearly black. Savannah pulled her gaze from Logan to apologize to the next person in line, her Southern manners coming out, and realized nearly everyone had scattered. Logan's trick had worked—in more ways than one. There was just one person left in line. Travis. And he made no show of going anywhere.

Logan glanced uncomfortably at the town's sheriff. "I have a lot of ones here," he said, nodding to the wad of bills.

Travis didn't move. "I've got nothing but time."

Logan stared at him. "You're the sheriff. Surely you've got something better to do."

"Nope."

"Fine. I'll give you ten bucks to walk," Logan said.

"Thanks, but no thanks." Travis edged closer to Savannah, and Logan put out his arms, clearly growing flustered.

"Twenty."

"No."

"Fifty."

Travis glared at him. "No."

"Damn it, man, what will it take?"

Travis's face curved up into a wicked grin. "You take my place in the dunk tank."

The dunk tank, likely full of very cold water, sat beside

the main stage, ready for Travis to climb inside. Logan eyed it and then Savannah.

"You don't have to do this," she said.

"Yeah...I do. I thought this was all a test, to see if you felt something. But the joke was on me." He shook his head slowly. "I can't do this anymore. Be around you everyday and act like it doesn't matter. Like we aren't more. Because we are so much more to me. God knows I'll never deserve your attention, but I'm far too weak a man to push it away. If you want this, then I'm here." He focused back on Travis and reached out to shake his hand. "Deal. I've already taken the plunge. Might as well see it through."

Savannah's chest warmed as she stared after him on his way to the dunk tank. Forget losing her heart by the end of the day. It was already gone.

Logan walked through the door of his room at the bed-and-breakfast, sopping wet but with a smile on his face all the same. After that last kiss with Savannah, he'd needed the cold water of the dunk tank before seeing her again, or else he might forget all logic and take her to his room, where he'd do a lot more than simply kiss her.

He'd spent the night before awake, staring at his door, curious if Savannah was awake in her room or sleeping, if she was thinking or dreaming. He thought of Will, and all the things Logan had done to try to live his life for his friend only to end every day miserable.

Well, he was tired of being miserable. He was sorry. God above, he would forever be sorry. But he couldn't deny his feelings for Savannah Hale any longer. He didn't just want her. He loved her. Through and through, he loved her. That kind of love deserved to be realized, to be said out loud, to be cultivated and grown. And if what Mrs. Cooke had hinted at was true, maybe Savannah felt something more for him, too.

Tugging off his shirt, he tossed it to the floor and reached for a fresh towel, not realizing he'd left his door open until a voice he'd recognize anywhere asked, "What just happened?"

He turned around to find Savannah standing in his doorway, half into his world and half out. He wanted to launch into every thought and feeling he had about her and them, but instead, he decided to tread cautiously. "Here in the States we call it kissing."

"So that's it. Just kissing?"

Never the timid sort, he pushed off his cargo shorts, exposing a pair of plaid boxers that stuck to his legs. Her gaze dropped, and she blanched, forever the timid sort. "No. It wasn't just kissing," Logan said. "And right now, it's taking all my effort to keep from proving how much more than *just kissing* I want this to be."

Her eyes snapped to him, and for a moment he thought she might come to him, but then she shook her head, her surprise turning to sadness. "I don't understand you. You said in the basement that you'd never been more sorry. Then you stand at my booth like a caveman, refusing to allow anyone else to kiss me."

"Did you want someone else to kiss you?"

"That's not the point."

Logan took a cautious step toward her. "I think it is."

The sky was dark now, the easiness of the day replaced with the moon and stars, all the makings of romance. All the things they weren't ready to explore. But maybe they'd never be ready, and maybe that didn't matter.

Savannah bit down on her bottom lip, and Logan groaned, missing the feel of it pressed against his own.

"You can't do that while you're talking to me unless you want this to get very awkward." His gaze dropped to his boxers, and her eyes widened, before a small laugh escaped those perfect lips.

"You're never embarrassed are you? Never shy."

Logan licked his own lips, immediately noting how much he wished he were licking hers. "We are who we are. No reason to dance around it like it's going to change."

"No."

"No, what?"

She peered at him through her lashes. "No, I didn't want anyone else to kiss me. Not then. And not now."

Like her words unlocked the final bolt in his restraint, Logan sprang forward, wrapping his arms around her and pressing his lips to hers like she was his lifeline and without her he would drown.

His fingers slid into her hair, stroking the waves as he slowed the kiss, enjoying the change, the sureness of knowing she wanted to kiss him back. This wasn't charity, which was exactly why he'd concocted his plan. He knew if she felt something for him, by the end of the day she wouldn't be able to stay away. Sex was impersonal. You could hook up and leave. But kissing had a depth to it that bound you to a person. A good kiss would last forever in your memory, and Savannah and Logan were made to kiss. It was natural and easy and all consuming. He knew that all those years ago, and it had scared the shit out of him.

But now, he wasn't a nineteen-year-old boy. He was a man, and he may never deserve to have her, but he had to try, or else he would regret it for the rest of his life.

She shivered in his arms and he pulled away, a small smile on his face at the disappointment on hers.

"Let's warm you up."

He closed the door to his room and took her hand in his, leading her to the bathroom, where he turned on the shower a little too hot, but he had a feeling they wouldn't notice the heat anyway.

Allowing the steam to fill the room, he took his time slipping off her tank top and helping her out of her shorts, his gaze travelling over every inch of exposed flesh. God, she was beautiful. He tugged her closer, his lips finding the dip of her neck, and she trembled, this time of something other than cold.

He stepped into the shower, which was full of steam and the smell of Irish Spring soap, the only kind he'd ever used. He reached for her hand, and without hesitation, she followed him under the water. His hands glided down her waist, over the swell of her hips and her skin bubbled up in goose bumps.

"Tell me you want this as badly as I do."

"I've wanted this for a long time." Her gaze lifted. "Long before I should have."

"You mean...?"

"You never noticed me, Logan Park. But I always noticed you."

Now he knew what Mrs. Cooke had said was true.

Savannah hadn't only loved Will...she cared for Logan. Maybe even loved him, too.

The revelation made him want to take her right then, but he didn't want to rush. Not now. Instead, he kissed her lips slowly, memorizing the way they felt and tasted, the sweet sounds she made. Then he went to her cheek, then her neck, then the swell of her breasts. Before long the weight on his shoulders lifted, the stone over his heart softened, and as they finally connected, he allowed himself to forget the past and simply enjoy the woman he loved.

Chapter Eleven

Savannah woke with a smile on her face and a single yellow rose from the garden on her pillow. Beneath it was a note, and scribbled across the paper in black ink were the words: *Went into town to grab breakfast. Be back soon. X Logan*

She took the note in her hand and pressed it to her chest, a thin sheet the only thing covering her body. They'd spent the night tangled up in each other, few words passing, and for once she didn't want to think about all the whys or ifs or hows. She just wanted to enjoy the feel of the man she wanted beside her.

Slipping out of bed, she put on her panties and tank top and tiptoed out of Logan's room in an effort to make it to hers without anyone noticing. Only the moment she closed the door and turned around, she ran smack into Jim—his tool belt around his waist, his hand on the ladder beside Logan's door, and a mix of humor and mortification on his face.

"Um, I…" Jim turned away. "I'll just go back the way I came." He covered his eyes with one hand and headed down the steps, leaving Savannah a tomato-red mess at the top of the steps.

"Fantastic. Now, I've scared off the only good handyman in town."

Just then the door beside Savannah's door opened, and Jack stopped mid-step. "Do you ever wear clothes?" He shook his head. "Go get ready before you scare our new guests."

Savannah felt her face light up. "Guests?"

He smiled back. "I switched the sign to open yesterday during the festival. Four couples stayed the night with plans to stay for the weekend."

"Oh my God. Jack!"

"Yeah, yeah. I'm amazing. I know. Now go get ready before you have the husbands ogling you and piss off all the wives."

"Thank you," she said, before disappearing into her room.

Savannah took her time in the shower, remembering her last one and the man she'd shared it with. They'd spent the night so engrossed in each other's bodies there wasn't time to stop and ask what they were doing, though Savannah wondered if she wanted to know. Sometimes things were better left open and unsaid, tucked away for a safer time.

The day was well on its way now, so Savannah dressed quickly and went downstairs, eager to take on her role as the manager of Maple Cove's Bed and Breakfast. Slipping behind the front desk and sorting the few papers that had been set there, she wondered when she'd decided to stay to run the B and B. She'd come home to sort things for her mother's funeral, but never once did she think she might actually enjoy being back in Maple Cove.

Before she could dwell on it, Hannah McGee walked through the front door, hair and makeup in perfect order. She wore a pink summer dress that hit at her knees, and apparently she'd misplaced her bra, because she surely wasn't wearing one. "Hey there, sweetie. How are you?" she asked.

"Fine." Savannah paused, curious if she'd missed something. "How are you?"

Hannah glanced around. "Oh, fine, fine. I was just curious if Logan was here."

"Actually, no. He's not." Savannah said, a little more smugly than she intended.

"I am now."

Savannah peered around Hannah, unable to keep the smile from her face as she took him in. He had on faded jeans and a red polo shirt that fit him so perfectly she wondered if he'd had it tailored. Unsure of what to expect, she nodded politely to him, then to Hannah. "You have a visitor."

He smiled back at her, holding her gaze for a second longer than he should and sending a flurry of butterflies through her belly. Then he turned his attention on Hannah. "What can I do for you?"

Hannah took a step toward him, standing far too close to be appropriate. They were in a place of business for heaven's sake. All right, so maybe that business involved beds and people sleeping, but still. Hannah didn't have a room here. Or did she?

Savannah picked up a pen from the desk and flicked it

a continuous rhythm as she searched for Hannah's name in the guestbook. Why didn't they have a computer here and software or something that recorded all of this stuff? She reached for her fix-it list and added: *Computer and registrations in a software or build something that would work in Excel.*

Her eyes lifted to Hannah and Logan, still talking away, and her pen started tapping against the wooden desk again, louder this time.

"Did you need something else, Hannah?" she asked, her smile so painted on it could have been a product of Maybelline's.

Her old friend turned to her and offered her own smile, before winking at Logan. "No. I got what I came for. See you in a few hours, Logan."

Suddenly the paperwork on the front desk looked very, very interesting. Savannah had set to sorting the stack, not registering or caring what was on the page, when Logan came in close and ran his hand over the small of her back and nuzzled her ear, sending a chill through her. Lord, how this man could drop her with one tiny touch.

"Good morning."

She didn't want to be some crazy jealous—what? She had no idea what they were, and she had no ownership over him. He could date whomever he like, including braless Hannah. So there. Take that, jealousy.

Stepping away from him, she went back to the stack. "I'm a little busy here."

Logan purposefully cocked his head to look at the papers. "Sorting a Toys 'R' Us ad?"

Savannah's eyes dropped and sure enough she was very

intently stacking a bunch of retail ads. Damn it.

"Well then." She set the stack aside and started for the kitchen. "I'm repainting the back trim today."

"All right. I'll help you."

She turned then, unable to hold her tongue. "Before or after you help Hannah McGee?"

A smile played at his lips as he edged toward her, his head slightly down in that sexy way as he watched her. "Am I sensing jealousy here?"

"No." Her hands went to her hips, but she looked away. "I don't care what you do."

"Is that right?"

"Yes."

Mrs. Cooke was setting out plates in the common room for the guests. Savannah didn't want to put on a show for her and have the woman second-guessing her. Not when Savannah had made her mind up that she wanted to stay and run the bed-and-breakfast. She felt sick to her stomach every time she thought about leaving. Now she just had to get the place fixed up and put out the word that it was open and ready for spring and summer business. And, of course, find a way to bring the mortgage current. Easy stuff.

"Savannah, look at me."

Releasing a slow breath, she forced her eyes over to Logan. "What?"

"There's only you. There's only ever been you."

"Really?"

He closed this distance between them, taking her hand and tugging her to him. "You have no idea." His mouth covered hers, sending a fresh flurry through her belly, before she heard someone clearing her throat.

"Sorry to bother you, honey," Mrs. Cooke said, smiling. "But I wanted to go over the menu for today."

Savannah kissed Logan once more and then stepped around him. "Of course."

"Should I get everything setup to paint the trim?" Logan asked.

"You'd do that?"

"Whatever you need."

Mrs. Cooke clucked her tongue from behind them. "Well, if you're offering services, maybe you could fix that basement doorknob. Someone's going to get stuck down there."

They burst out laughing, and Logan said, "I'm on it, Mrs. Cooke."

Savannah stared after Logan, enjoying the way his jeans fit from behind. She'd have to ask him to wear jeans more often.

"It's nice to see you smiling." Mrs. Cooke squeezed her shoulder, then started toward the kitchen, beckoning Savannah to follow. "And don't you let town gossip hurt your heart. You be happy, honey. Nobody can fault you for wanting to be happy."

"Wait, what do you mean town gossip?"

Mrs. Cooke's forehead wrinkled as she looked at her, then her expression relaxed and she shook her head. "Oh, I didn't realize…well, then never mind. Ignore me."

"No, please. Has someone said something about the bed-and-breakfast?" Savannah worried that rumors of the bed-and-breakfast's financial troubles had circulated. She didn't want the Hale name tarnished by her inability to save the business.

"No, nothing about the B and B, dear. Business is business and everyone's been there."

Savannah eyed her cautiously. "Then what?"

Mrs. Cook's eyes drifted out the back kitchen door to Logan, now sans shirt and sorting paint cans.

"Oh."

"But don't you worry over a little gossip. Maple will talk about the moon if it doesn't shine bright enough."

"Right." Savannah bit her lip and stared after Logan, her shoulders curling in. She'd always hated rumors, and the idea of being a piece of town gossip made her insides turn sour. She knew if she looked in the mirror she'd see the stress line between her eyebrows, which her mama had always tried to rub out.

Mrs. Cooke reached up and ran her thumb easily between Savannah's eyebrows, causing a warm feeling to move through her. "Now, now, that'll stick if you're not careful. You don't worry yourself about this. Be happy. That is the single best thing you can do to honor your parents."

Nodding, Savannah pushed aside the nagging doubts in her mind. She did deserve to be happy. "So the menu?"

"Right here."

Once she'd worked out the breakfast, lunch, and dinner menus, she pushed out the back French doors, only to find several women out on the deck, their eyes trained on Logan. She had to laugh.

"Looks like you have some admirers."

Logan swiped a bead of sweat off his forehead with the back of his arm, and Savannah could have sworn she heard an audible sigh from the ladies. "I hadn't noticed. Lately, there's only one admirer I'm interested in having." His gaze hit hers, and the fluttering in her stomach returned, her chest warming as their eyes locked. Would she ever get tired of this feeling? No, never.

Forget town gossip, she was about to jump the man and lose the only guests they had. Clearing her throat before her thoughts showed, she peered up at the trim around the kitchen and back double doors, all three of which led onto the deck. Logan had the brushes and paint pans set up and had already run blue painter's tape around the house itself in case they made any mistakes, which, with Savannah on the job, was very likely to happen.

Pulling her hair back into a ponytail, she grabbed a paintbrush and went for the trim, but Logan reached out a hand to stop her. "What are you doing?"

"Um, painting? What does it look like?"

Logan's expression turned serious. "You can't paint with a brush. You have to use the small roller, and the brush for the corners."

"That's ridiculous. They call them paintbrushes for a reason. They paint stuff. Including this trim."

"Everyone knows that if you paint with a brush you'll have lines from the bristles. That won't happen with a roller."

"He's right," one of the women chimed in, and Savannah nearly said, *of course you think he's right!* All eight of his abs were out for all to see. Add to that those low-hanging jeans and no shoes, and no woman in the world would argue with him right now. Well, other than Savannah, apparently.

A woman with a cropped blond bob sat up. "I agree with the girl. It doesn't matter what you use as long as you prime first. Are you priming?"

Savannah stared at the cans of paint with concern. "Oh.

I don't know." Her eyes lifted to Logan. "Are we priming?"

He smirked. "Admit I'm right, and I'll tell you."

"This is ridiculous. It's just painting. I could already be done." She dipped her brush, unsure if it was paint or primer or glue for all she knew, but at this point she had to wipe that grin off his face. What did it matter anyway? Wasn't primer white? She'd just double coat it or something.

"You can't do that," he said, his arms crossed now, all Very Serious Logan.

"Watch me." She started for the trim just as Logan darted in front of her, causing the brush to collide with his chest instead of the trim. Savannah's eyes went wide, a giggle fighting its way up her throat. "Sorry, I…" Logan glanced down slowly at the white stripe across his chest, and the giggle turned to full-out laughter.

"Think that's funny, do you?" he asked.

"No. It's freaking hilarious." She broke into fits, and Logan snatched the brush from her hand, swiping it across her cheek before she could move. "Hey!"

He shrugged. "Not my fault you're slow."

Savannah growled in answer, and the war began. The ladies rushed inside as Logan and Savannah took brushes and rollers, each jabbing at the other until they were both laughing loudly and coated in white paint—or primer. She still didn't know.

Finally, Logan snatched her as she went for his hair, and twisted her so her back was against his chest, his arms locked around her. "Surrender or suffer the ultimate punishment. Death by paint."

She wriggled in his arms, but he tightened his hold. No other choice in view, she gripped the handle of her brush and edged it dangerously close to the crotch of his jeans. In truth, it was the only spot she could reach. "I'm pretty sure you want to let me go."

"I'm pretty sure I never want to let you go," he whispered, and just like that, she dropped the brush, her body boneless. Logan's breath hit her neck in short bursts, his heart hammering against her back. "Too much too soon?"

She turned in his arms, her face close to his. "No. And I think that's what scares me the most." They fell into silence as he touched his forehead to hers. "Do me a favor, Logan Park?"

"Whatever you want, Savannah Hale."

"Don't leave."

He kissed her lips gently. "I'm not going anywhere."

Chapter Twelve

Logan stepped back to look at his creation, smiling at the effort and how well it had turned out. And if he'd timed it right, Savannah would be stepping outside, right about —

"Hey, Mrs. Cooke said you were looking for me? I was — "

He turned around to see her staring down at him from the deck, the lights from inside shining over her and making her appear dangerously close to an angel. Her mouth fell open and Logan took another step away from the blanket, his hands outstretched.

"Care to join me?"

A small smile tugged at her lips as she started down the steps, and as she walked toward him, tiny pieces of grass clung to her sandaled feet. He wondered if the grass was still too wet from the rain they'd had the day before, but there was supposed to be a lunar eclipse and he didn't want to miss it.

The night sky was already dark above them, the stars

impossibly bright against the black, without any cloud cover to hide them.

"Wine?" he asked as he poured a glass for her and then set it down beside his on the serving tray.

"I can't believe you did this." She took a seat beside him, and though he knew the grass must have soaked through to her clothes, she didn't say anything. Savannah had never been the sort of girl to care about those things, and it was one of the many things he loved about her.

He thought of that word—love—and how little he knew of Savannah today. Could he still say he loved her when he didn't really know her? Inside, he wasn't sure he'd ever stopped loving her, but if this was going to work, and God did he ever hope it would, they needed to go slow. Get to know one another again. He needed to romance her, so she would fall in love with him, and him her, as though for the very first time. And in a way, it was. At least, the first time he'd allowed himself to care for her without Will's ghost staring over his shoulder, judging him. But he'd spent his entire adult life trying to make up for Will's death, and while he would always love his best friend, he couldn't deny himself Savannah any longer.

They settled back on the blanket, enjoying their wine and the clear, warm night.

"What does twenty-eight-year-old Logan do for fun?"

He smiled. "You mean besides this? I work a lot. My assistant tries to get me out of the office at a decent hour and rarely succeeds."

"Wow. Assistant."

"Chloe. You'll have to meet her sometime when you come to Atlanta. You'd like her."

Savannah's head turned toward him, the small smile returning. "*When* I come to Atlanta?"

"I hope you will. Of course, if you go back to Boston then—"

"I think I want to stay."

"You do?"

She lay back on the blanket, her hands resting on her stomach as she crossed her ankles and stared up at the sky. "I don't think it will be easy, but my parents loved this place. They worked their entire lives to make it thrive. Sure, they made some mistakes, but there are people who love the B and B, people who come every year, who would be devastated if we sold."

Logan cleared his throat and took another long sip of his wine. There were only two subjects he'd hoped to avoid with her tonight. Will was one and the bed-and-breakfast was the other. The partners intended for him to close this deal, and he'd had little guilt about that fact. Savannah had her own life in Boston. He never dreamed she'd want to come back and take the place over, but now...

"I know nothing about running it. It's so far behind on the mortgage that I don't know if I'll even be able to save it, but I have to try. For them. For myself. I'll regret it forever if I don't." She laughed then. "You must think I'm crazy. Who fights for something that's already gone?"

" I don't think you're crazy. I think it's what they would want you to do. It's brave."

"You think so?"

"It's what I'd do if I were you."

And there it was, him putting her before his job. He shouldn't support this. He should offer all the reasons why selling was a good idea—the money, the stress relief, her job and life back in Boston—but none of those things came to his mind. Because the truth was, he'd worked for years now and had made himself a small fortune and not once had he ever felt as happy as Savannah looked when she was talking with a guest. That kind of happiness should be nurtured not diminished.

She rolled her head toward him, watching him for a moment before speaking. "And what about you? Have you ever considered moving back? Opening a business here like you always dreamed?"

The stars were bright tonight, the air comfortable, with not a sound around them, making it easy to relax enough to be honest, something Logan rarely allowed himself to do. "Maybe one day. I have some things to check off my list first."

The conversation was veering dangerously close to Will now, and the last thing he wanted was to make her remember all the reasons they shouldn't be together. A smell of fresh rain still lingered in the air, and as Logan drew it in, he wondered if he could live in Maple again. With Savannah around, it might be worth the occasional run-in with his dad.

"Check off?"

"There are just certain things I need to do in my life."

"Like what?"

Logan had the list so memorized it appeared in his mind without any effort at all. "Like snowboarding."

She turned her head toward him again, a wide grin forming. "You want to go snowboarding."

"Something like that."

"What else do you want to do?"

Logan's mouth set into a hard line as he thought about her question. He had never been the kind of person to plan out his life. He lived by the moment up until Will died, and then he no longer felt like his life belonged to him. If he could do anything at all, would he want to snowboard? Would that make his list? Maybe. Or maybe not.

"What do I want to do or what do I need to do?"

Her eyebrows knit together, and he wondered if she could see into his mind, pick out the pieces that were his and those that were Will's. He'd worried for a long time that when he finally saw Savannah again he would've become too much like Will for her to ever see him clearly. But then, he'd never been able to be anyone but himself with her.

"What do you need to do?" Her voice was low as she asked the question, like she knew there was something more to the conversation, but she didn't want to search it out. Not yet.

"Snowboard. Visit Africa. Backpack through Asia. Earn an MBA...and five million dollars."

She sat up and peered down at him. He'd placed his hands behind his head as he ticked off the last five things on the list. He'd planned to knock out Africa and Asia when he hit Europe after his second tour in Iraq, but then he was offered the job with Hartridge and Long, and he figured he better get started on the five million if he hoped to get there in his lifetime.

At the time, it seemed an impossible number, but he was very good at his job and he was already halfway there thanks to an impressive salary, an even more impressive bonus plan, and a few smart investments. Savannah was right, he was a numbers man through and through, and his love of statistics had served him well.

If only money were enough.

He'd been on both sides of the coin—dirt poor as a kid and quite wealthy as an adult—and through it all only one thing had remained constant. Savannah. Which was why he refused to push her away now.

She opened her mouth and closed it, likely deciding which of the list she wanted to ask him about first, and he was relieved when she said, "You have a double major. Why bother with the MBA? Seems like a waste."

He laughed. "Yeah, probably is. You went to Boston College, right? What was your major?"

"Journalism," she said with a hint of longing in her voice. "I wanted to be one of those freelancers that travels to wild and dangerous places, and then big magazines would publish my stories."

"And what happened?" As soon as the words slipped out, he wanted to take them back. He knew what had happened. Will. She'd been a year into college when she came home that summer and Logan delivered the worst news of her life. It made sense that she wouldn't want to risk her life after losing someone to war.

They fell into silence, and she lay back down beside him, her thoughts so evident they were almost tangible.

"Ask," he said finally.

"I'm sorry, I just...none of those things sound like you. I wouldn't have put any of them on your list. Maybe I don't know you as well as I thought I did, but I don't think that's it. I think there's more to your list than you're telling me. Am I right?"

Logan didn't want to respond her question, so instead

he asked one of his own. "What *would* be on my list?" He turned his head so he could see her when she answered.

A falling star dropped from the night, and they watched it in silence, losing themselves to the greatness of the sky, the bubbling sound of a nearby fountain the only thing to keep them grounded on Earth. Logan realized then that when people said, "this is the life," they meant moments like this.

"Spear fishing."

He glanced over to Savannah. "What?"

"Your list. I think you'd have spear fishing on it. Deep down in the Atlantic, sharks all around you, but you wouldn't care. And you'd choose Italy and France over Asia and Africa, but you wouldn't be able to decide where to visit first so you'd make me pick."

"And what would you choose?" he whispered, caught up in her tale of his life.

"Rome, so you could see the Sistine Chapel. You always loved art."

He did, though he'd never admitted as much to anyone.

"And I'd never have guessed you cared about money enough to want thousands let alone millions."

He didn't. Money was trivial to him, and he'd become a spender because of it. The only reason he saved at all was to hit the stupid five million goal.

Eyes back on the night sky, the eclipse happening before them, Logan's thoughts became strained. He'd expected them to need to relearn one another, but maybe a person's core never changed. And if that were the case and neither of them was different, did that mean their struggles were the same? Would they forever live under the shadow of Will's death?

"What would make your list?" Logan asked, though he thought maybe he knew the answer. Still, he wanted to hear her say it—see if he knew her as well as he thought.

She reached out for his hand, threading her fingers through his. "I'd never make a list," she said. "And neither would you."

Rolling onto his side and propping up on one elbow, he brushed her hair from her face, desperate to be closer to this woman who saw straight into the depths of him. "No, I wouldn't." And then he leaned down, sealing his mouth over hers as he let his mind and the past drift away, leaving only the two of them under a star covered night. And then he thought, if he had made a list, surely this moment would have been on it.

Chapter Thirteen

The sky was blue. The clouds white. The sun bright as ever. Not at thing in the world could wreck Savannah's mood. One week of perfection with Logan and suddenly she didn't know which way was right and which was left, but as long as Logan was ahead of her, she'd follow along.

Of course, most of their time together had been around the B and B, without half the town eyeing their every move. And though Mrs. Cooke said talk had already started up about them, Savannah hadn't seen or heard it first hand. She liked to pretend it was like the whole tree falling in the forest thing. If you're not there to hear it, the sound doesn't exist. Same with gossip.

At least that was what she told herself as she entered Dan's Dixie Store. She walked around to the produce aisle to pick up some apples to make an apple pie. She'd been killing herself trying to think of a creative idea to bring in new business at the bed-and-breakfast, but had come up empty.

She needed to cook to get her brain juices moving again, and she'd been craving apple pie with vanilla bean ice cream all week. The day was closing in when she'd have no choice but to try to get a loan to cover what the bed-and-breakfast needed, or ask her brother for a loan. A part of her was angry that he hadn't offered outright. He was a professional athlete! Surely that meant he had plenty of extra money, but every time she attempted to bring it up, he changed the subject, all but saying he had no interest in helping the bed-and-breakfast out of its hole. Leigh was a museum curator with a hopelessly small salary, so Savannah hadn't even asked her, though she knew Leigh would help if she could. So that left Savannah to figure it out on her own.

"Hey there, stranger."

Savannah turned to see Hannah and Dana standing close by, clearly with something on their minds. For a grocery run, they were overly dressed, making her feel less and less like she belonged in their circle. Savannah tried to remember why she'd ever been friends with them.

"We heard you were having volunteers over to help with a few projects. We'd be happy to help."

Ah, man. Here she was thinking the worst of them, and they were just trying to be nice. She was a horrible person, who should repent her judgments to God...along with her four uses of God and seven uses of Jesus C yesterday. Or maybe she'd just say *sorry for everything I've ever done that might be considered a sin* and call it a day.

"That would be great," Savannah said, edging closer to them. "We're working in the garden later today. Maybe you could—"

"Is Logan going to be there? I mean, surely he is, right?

After all, y'all are an item aren't you?"

So much for nice.

"I don't really know if he will. Probably."

"Fantastic. We were eager to see you two together in the flesh. Talk has it you've been hiding out," Dana said. "Though, if it is all just a rumor, would you let me know? I wouldn't mind asking Logan out." She grinned. "You know...if you won't mind?"

"Sure," Savannah said through gritted teeth. Thankfully that seemed to appease them, and they went on their way.

So, clearly they were still in high school. Though she didn't remember either of them giving Logan a second glance back then. Sure, he'd had his looks, but he was from the wrong side of the tracks, his father or mother always the source of some type of town gossip. They didn't see Logan for the person he was then and likely didn't now, either.

Her thoughts drifted back to the lunar eclipse, a romantic evening under the stars. That was Logan—all crooked grin on the outside, but inside lay a man who knew how to sweep a woman away. If only she could spend every evening under the stars.

She stopped walking, her mind turning the phrase over and over again. A romantic evening under the stars. What if the bed-and-breakfast offered something like that for its guests? What if they coordinated romantic picnics under the stars—or just wine like Logan had planned for her? And maybe she could have a screen brought in on Fridays and show old movies. Or have a live band.

Pushing her cart to the checkout as fast as possible, ignoring the sidelong looks from people as she passed, she called Leigh.

"Are you at the bed-and-breakfast?"

"Yes. Where else would I be? You have me running the front desk."

Savannah ignored her sister's snark and continued on. "Good. Grab Jack. I'll be there in five."

There were people seated out in the garden as Savannah walked by, and she waved to them cheerfully. "Having a nice stay?"

"The best. Thank you, dear."

Her heart expanded in her chest. Maybe Logan was right. She did love the bed-and-breakfast, loved interacting with guests, loved choosing the menu. She loved building memories for other people, watching their faces light up as they arrived. How could she go back to a corporate job after this?

She couldn't.

Dangerous ideas poked at her brain, tempting her to make plans she had no right to make. Plans with her family back together, running the bed-and-breakfast. Plans with Logan by her side.

Shaking off the thought before hope gave way to crazy, she nodded to Leigh. "One second. Let me set down these bags." Mrs. Cooke took them off her hands in the kitchen, and she went back to the front.

"I have an idea. What if we start a romance under the stars theme? We can have laundered plush blankets, wooden serving trays, and wine and goblets for each couple. We can even serve food out there for them. Maybe one night we have live music. Maybe another we can rent a screen and show old movies. It would give us a theme. People would know they would get a special time when they came here."

Leigh chewed at her black-painted nails, and then she dropped her arms and grinned. "I like it. We can create a Facebook page and even run a few ads to get the word out. This could work."

Both girls turned to their brother, who just stared out the front windows. "Jack?"

"What?"

"What do you think?" Leigh asked, clearly growing frustrated with her brother.

"I think it costs money to run ads and the bed-and-breakfast is already in the red."

Savannah bit her lip. *Now or never.* "Well, I was kind of hoping to talk to you about that. I thought maybe you could—"

"No." He turned for the steps, but Savannah was the oldest of the Hale kids and she wasn't going to be cut off by her little brother, even if he was a foot taller than her.

"What do you mean 'no'? We need you."

Jack shook his head. "There's nothing I can do."

"You aren't even trying. Mama and Daddy loved this place. It was everything to them. Don't you care? Don't you care about anyone but yourself? I'm not asking you to buy the place. I'm asking you to help continue our parents' legacy. Please."

Jack's gaze landed on Savannah, his voice full of defeat. "You don't understand what I'm saying, Anna. There's nothing I *can* do."

"But—"

"I'm broke."

The words hung in the air between them, dirty and disheartening. "But how is that possible. You're a pro athlete.

Surely your salary is…" Savannah trailed off at the look on his face.

"Mom knew. She'd been pushing me to get help for the last few years."

"Help with what?"

He released a long breath, like he'd been holding it his whole life and only now had remembered to exhale. "I have a gambling problem. It started several years ago and finally came to a head just before Mom died. Now I'm out for a year, maybe longer. I bet on a game."

"I don't understand. Gambling's a problem, but it's not illegal."

"It goes against rule twenty-one for a player to bet on a baseball game. Any game. If it's a bet against a game the player isn't involved in, then the player's ineligible for a year. If it's a game the player was set to play in, then he's permanently ineligible."

"Oh my God."

Jack ran a hand through his hair. "I'm sorry I can't help. Sorry for screwing up my life. Sorry it's ended up hurting the family."

Unable to bear the weight of losing the last shot she had, Savannah slumped down onto the top step, tears welling in her eyes though she wouldn't let them fall. Not yet. Frank had told her she had two more weeks, but how could she earn enough to keep the house from foreclosure?

"What if we took out a loan?" she said.

Jack laughed sarcastically. "Do you really want to talk credit scores with me? Maybe you could get a loan."

"I had the bank try yesterday. I was denied, and Leigh doesn't have enough credit to qualify."

"So what do we do?"

The light streamed in from the oval window in the two-story foyer, hitting Savannah directly in the face. For a moment she felt angry—at her meager savings, at her brother's gambling, at her mother for allowing the bed-and-breakfast to get into this mess. She wanted to shout at the light to get out of her face, let her cry in the shadows for once. But the sun refused to let up, and that's when Savannah realized neither did her mother.

Jane had mortgaged the house again and again to help the bed-and-breakfast stay afloat, and she wouldn't have given it up without exhausting every possible option.

Savannah thought her romance under the stars idea was a good one. Good enough to pull them out of this mess? Maybe with a little creative play with their cash flow, it just might be a start.

"We'll work harder," Savannah finally said to her brother. "We need the volunteers here today and tomorrow to finish up the last of the projects on the list. I'll have Leigh create the Facebook page, run a few ads, and contact radio stations for ad costs. We'll use every dollar we make to try to save it."

"Do you think it will work?"

Starting down the steps with new determination, she said, "It has to," before pushing up her shirtsleeves and heading out the front door. Time to save the bed-and-breakfast, even if it took every ounce of sweat and tears she had to do it.

Logan turned down the dirt road to his parents' house, bile climbing his throat with each passing second. His care for Savannah was the only reason he was there, and while she'd never ask him to seek out his father, Logan knew she needed a landscaper and there was only one in town.

They had two days to do a lot of work in the garden of the bed-and-breakfast, and though Logan's dad was a piece of shit father and husband and man, he was a damn good landscaper. It was the one thing he'd done right in his life, and with any luck, he'd agree to help them get the gardens ready for Friday's debut of Maple Cove's Romance Under the Stars.

Asking Canton Park for help would be one of the hardest things Logan had ever done, but he told himself that no matter what his father said, it didn't change who Logan was today. His father's words were just that—words. They couldn't touch him now.

The once white house resembled an old, dying zebra. Brown, rotted wood ran side-by-side with the white. One of the windows had been broken and was covered with a black trash bag. Several shingles from the roof had blown off from one of the many summer thunderstorms Maple saw, likely creating a leak somewhere in the house that his father would never fix.

Logan wondered if his mother took one look at the run-down house, the angry drunk inside, her son fighting a war a world away, and decided she couldn't do it anymore. Or if she'd broken up yet another marriage and ran off with the sleaze. He didn't know, but he liked to think a person could change—he certainly had—and it gave him a bit of comfort to think at least one of his parents had become a good person after all the bad.

As though on cue, Canton Park pushed open his screen door, letting it rap loudly behind him, a half-smoked cigarette dangling from his lips. Gray sprinkled his greasy black hair and, like always, he wore a white V-neck undershirt, worn khaki pants, and a sneer at finding his son before him. No amount of time could turn this man good.

"Nice truck. You steal it?" He chuckled, but the laugh was quickly replaced by a hacking, emphysema-related cough.

Pushing aside the insult—there would be more before he made it off the property—Logan asked, "Can I come in?" His voice sounded weaker to his ears than he liked, but even as a man a part of him would always be Canton Park's boy.

His father considered him. "If you're here for money, I ain't—"

"I'm not here for money." Even the suggestion pissed Logan off. He'd never once asked him for anything, taking a job for Jim senior when he turned thirteen, and it'd been a chore to keep the cash he earned back then from his father's greedy hands. The question proved just how little his father knew of Logan today, which stung despite Logan's efforts to guard his feelings. "I came to offer you a job."

"Well, come in already. I don't got all day."

Drawing a long breath for patience, Logan stepped inside his childhood home. Memories hit him immediately. The forever cloud of smoke in the living room. The black spot on the linoleum floor in the kitchen, where Canton (drunk as always) had poured liquor on Logan's Army T-shirt and set fire to it, laughing as he asked if his son was brave now. That was the last day he'd seen his father, the last day he'd ever planned to see him. Being there again felt like a physical assault.

The TV sat in the center of the room, the orange couch still had the same indentations in it where Canton passed out there at night, never quite making it to his room.

"What's this about a job?"

Logan sat down on the couch, wishing he could have had someone else hire his father. Jack or Leigh. But he couldn't explain to them why he didn't want to go there himself. Savannah knew a little, but only Will had known the depths of Logan's upbringing.

"The bed-and-breakfast in town needs some help in their garden and maybe a few things surrounding it."

Canton lit another cigarette. "I don't work for free."

"I'll pay you. Half now. Half when the job is done." His father might be a good landscaper, but he didn't trust him to fulfill any agreement he made with Logan. "The only thing I ask is that you don't mention the money when you're there. Just tell them you're doing it for free."

His eyebrow cocked as he blew out a long puff of smoke, followed by a single cough as though his body no longer knew how to breathe without coughing. "Why would I do that?"

"Here's the first half," Logan said, setting down five hundred dollars on the end table. "I figured a thousand should cover it."

"Is this about that Hale girl you used to be sweet on? What would that girl want with a piece of shit like you? You'll never learn will you? Girls like that want respectable men who can commit. You couldn't even commit to the military. Did your time and got the hell out. So much for serving your country. What is it you do now to have a thousand dollars to fork out?"

Logan kept his mouth shut. He'd spent five years in the army, risking his life more times than he could count. He would never claim he was the bravest, but damned if he'd allow someone to lessen what he'd done for America in that time. Instead he stood, eager to get the hell out of there. "Ah, this and that. Do we have a deal or not?"

"Another five hundred when I'm done? Plus the cost of materials."

Logan counted out another three hundred onto the table. "That should cover materials and whatever plants you need. Be there tomorrow at nine. Sober." Then he walked out of the house where he was raised, praying he'd never have to return.

Chapter Fourteen

The moon rose high above them, full and vibrant, casting its own light down on the scene. Savannah sighed as she took another glance around the grounds where they had everything set up for Romance Under the Stars. A smile of pride spread across her face.

Already there were five couples seated on plaid blankets, all red with white and green crisscrossing lines, and fringe on all four sides. The gardens cradling the plot of land where they'd decided to position the event were overflowing with blooming bushes and tulips and lilies. Spaced every few feet were large metal lanterns, immersed into the gardens like they'd grown from the ground up, and soft music played in the speakers hidden within the greenery. The whole effect was enchanting and oh so romantic.

Canton had done an amazing job, all at no charge, which made Savannah wonder if he'd turned his life around. Maybe he'd given up the bottle, decided to live his life for someone other than himself—like for his son. She wasn't sure, but she knew better than to ask. Logan revealed the depths of his life in his own way and in his own time. She wouldn't push him.

"Savannah, honey," Mrs. Cooke said from the kitchen door, wearing her best pearl earrings and her hair swept back in a fashionable bun. Everyone dressed well tonight. "There are three couples asking to eat under the stars. I didn't know if you wanted to show them out?"

"I do, thank you." Savannah dashed back inside, her white skirt dancing around her calves as she walked, her black, strappy heels clacking against the hardwood floors. A simple black sleeveless blouse completed her look, and she decided that if she could pull this off and save the bed-and-breakfast she would make black and white her signature look while at work.

The smell of roasted chicken hit her nose as she passed the kitchen, causing her stomach to rumble. A promise to stop for lunch had turned into dinner, and she made a mental note to ask Mrs. Cooke to make her a plate for later.

She clasped her hands together as she walked into the grand foyer, her eyes sparking with excitement as she took in the line of guests. "Welcome to Maple Cove's Bed and Breakfast, we're happy you're with us to—" Savannah stopped short at the sight of the second couple in the row.

The man was tall, with cropped gray and white hair and a slight hunch from working over a computer all his life. Beside him stood a petite woman with black hair that'd never once been dyed, yet still showed signs of her age. Simple makeup complemented her face, but as her eyes met Savannah's, she beamed.

"Oh, honey, I have missed your sweet face." She walked to Savannah and pulled her into the sort of hug that would have made Savannah smile if it weren't for the fact that she was trying very hard not to throw up. With stinging eyes, she drew a breath, then two, for strength, and took a step back to take in Patricia and William Pruitt. Will's parents. They must have returned from Europe.

"Can you give me one second?" she said to them, then went to the front desk and whispered for Leigh to take care of the other guests. Leigh's eyebrows rose in question until she caught sight of the Pruitts. She nodded and took the other four couples away. Four! That made nine couples already and the night had just begun. Clearly, Leigh's work advertising the event had proven worth the money they'd thrown together to pay for it. She'd need to thank her later. If they managed to save the place, Leigh would make an amazing events coordinator. The thought sent butterflies through her stomach, and she said a little prayer that God would give her this one second chance. All right, two. This and…Logan.

As though he heard his name called in her thoughts, he walked through the front door. Instantly, a smile spread across his face and her skin hummed in answer. It was as if the moment he entered a room, all the tension she held so tightly melted away. He made her feel like anything was possible, his strong arms and warm eyes ready to carry her through the worst of whatever happened.

"Hey," she said, unable to hide her excitement at seeing him and not caring in the least.

"Hey yourself, gorgeous." He leaned toward her just as something over her shoulder caught his eye from, and she knew without him having to say anything that he'd seen the

Pruitts.

"They're here for dinner," she said, trying to calm the storm she saw brewing in his eyes. Only this wasn't something that words could settle. This was all misery, a wound that would never heal, no matter what she said. "Logan, look at me."

But she knew he couldn't. Instead he hugged her like she were his little sister, and then stepped as far away from her as possible.

Savannah tried to push aside the ache in her chest at his reaction. He was trying to spare the Pruitts' feelings. How could she be upset? Only this didn't feel like a simple act of kindness. This felt like a completely different Logan. The kind, compassionate businessman she knew transformed to a broken soldier before her very eyes. And maybe that was life for a soldier. Maybe their fatigues would forever remain tattooed to their bodies, right below their civilian clothes, never vanishing no matter how hard they scrubbed their skin.

"Mr. and Mrs. Pruitt," he said, forever the gentleman. He walked around the desk to them, shaking Mr. Pruitt's hand then hugging Mrs. Pruitt, and all Savannah could do was watch, her eyes burning so badly she had to swallow several times to keep her emotions at bay.

Lifting her head, she walked over to join them, feeling less and less like she belonged there.

"I was just telling Logan that I would love to have you both over for lunch before he heads back to Atlanta and you to Boston," Mrs. Pruitt said. "Will would have loved to see you were friends now." Her voice cracked only once when she said Will's name, but otherwise she showed nothing but genuine happiness at seeing them.

Logan's eyes found the wall beside them, and though he nodded once, he was no longer with them. Maybe he was back in Afghanistan. Maybe Iraq. Maybe at Will's funeral. Savannah couldn't be sure, but he wasn't with her. And what scared her most was that she didn't know if this was one blip on their relationship map or if it would be like this forever. A giant step back for every inch they took forward. Would every reminder of Will have him retreating?

She didn't know, but she did know that she couldn't handle him leaving her again. Losing Will had almost broken her, and then Logan right after was enough to make her question how she would ever continue.

She did, but only by leaving town and never ever looking back.

Logan felt like all the air had been sucked from his body by a tornado, his skin pricking like even it wanted to escape. He watched Will's parents sit down on their blanket in the gardens, Mr. Pruitt pouring a glass of wine for Mrs. Pruitt, and then the sweet smile on her face as she accepted it. They deserved nothing but happiness, and damn if he wasn't the asshole who'd gone and moved in on Will's girl, the one person they still viewed as a means to their son. He wanted to punch himself, but then Savannah returned from showing them to their spot, and he could see the hurt on her face before she'd even said a word. There was no winning here.

"Can I speak to you please?" she asked.

The main dining area was crowded with people, the bed-and-breakfast at full capacity. Logan would have grinned with pride, if he weren't wishing he could be somewhere else. He thought of the Pruitts out on the lawn, their opinion of him forever golden, and then of Savannah looking at him like he held her pure heart in his dirty palms. For Christ's sake, he was here to take over her family's business. She should hate him. She should push him away and tell him never to return, as she had those first few days. This…this was just…

"I need to make a call." He heard himself say the words, but even as they left him he wished he could reel them back in like a bad cast. Still, he couldn't bring himself to do anything else. He felt his body shutting down, his heart closing up, steel slipping over his skin and bones, replacing the warmth with cold.

When he'd joined the army, they'd taught him to leave his old self behind. Those weeks in basic training were meant to breakdown the image he held of himself and replace *one*, singular, with *unit,* plural. He was no longer a singular vessel, but a part of something greater.

It had taken Logan a long time to shake the feeling of worthlessness once he left the army, and even now, there were moments he questioned the importance of his life. He pushed aside his negative thoughts most of the time, because while he wasn't on a mission to support the freedoms of the American people, he was living out his best friend's greatest wishes. Surely that meant something.

But Will hadn't wished for his best friend to be with the love of his life. Still, how was it Logan's fault that he and Will fell for the same girl? How was it his fault that

Will called dibs first? It wasn't like he could turn off those feelings. He might have been a soldier, but he was also just a man, trying his best to do what was right and failing at every turn. Vowing to never fail again, he'd left Savannah. Left all those old feelings behind. Only to end up right back in the nightmare.

He was a fool.

"A call. At this hour." It wasn't a question and her tone was enough to make him want to ask her for forgiveness. For her to forget the stupid comment and sink into him the way she did, like he and he alone could shield her from the world.

But he couldn't bring himself to look at her. "I have a demanding job. They call me when they want something, and they require me to respond. I don't expect you to understand."

"What is that supposed to mean?"

He looked pointedly at her now, allowing his anger at himself to take over his logic. "You've been here nearly a month, Savannah. What company on the planet would allow that kind of leave for someone vital to their organization?" *Please, God, kick me in the teeth now before I do any more damage.*

"So, you're saying because my company allowed me an extended leave that I can't possibly be important to them? It couldn't at all be that I have an amazing boss, who herself lost her mother last year? That she allowed me to take a week for bereavement, plus all the vacation time I needed? That I work every night making sure my job is covered and no emails are going untouched? No, that wouldn't at all make sense to you would it? You've never thought of any one other than yourself your entire life."

Her words hit him square in the chest. Of all the people in his life, all the people he knew, he never thought she was fooled by the image he portrayed. He thought she saw more, saw deeper, and the realization that she was like everyone else hurt more than he could have imagined.

"I didn't say that."

"No, but you were thinking it."

He didn't deny what she said, mainly because at this point he wanted her angry as much as he wanted himself to be angry. Anger produced results. Other emotions weren't so easy to process.

The sky had darkened to black, nothing out except the full moon to stare down on them. like even it judged him and his horrid actions. He walked down the front steps, Savannah beside him, and he desperately wanted to ask her to turn back. At the moment, his mind wasn't thinking clearly enough to have this conversation. Any second he could ruin everything, and he still didn't know if that was exactly what he needed or the worst thing that could possibly happen to him. The war between his mind and heart waged on.

Savannah stopped a few yards down the drive, her arms wrapped around herself. He couldn't see her face clearly in the dark, but he didn't need to. Her thoughts were clear.

"Just do it now."

His teeth ground together as he stared into the trees cradling the drive, every muscle in his body aching from the effort not to go to her. "Do what?"

"Say good-bye. Do it now." Her eyes lifted to his, tears brimming on her lashes, threatening to rain. "I can't take you leaving again without a good-bye. I at least deserve that."

"Savannah…"

"Just do it!" she cried.

He peered down into the face of the woman he loved, his heart shattering into tiny pieces. "I can't."

She shook her head and wiped away a stray tear then turned back to the bed-and-breakfast, and all he could do was watch her go, not strong enough to stop her and sure as hell not strong enough to leave.

Once she slipped inside the door, he pulled his phone from his pocket, prepared to text Leigh to look after her, but saw a new voicemail from the office. He clicked it and lifted his phone to his ear, his body going numb with each word.

"Logan? It's Alan. Bill and I will be in Maple Cove tomorrow to look at the bed-and-breakfast. Meet us there at nine."

Chapter Fifteen

Savannah woke to a cold bed and nothing but the sound of her hammering heart to keep her company. She'd dreamed about her and Logan's first kiss, the rain all around them, his face etched with regret as soon as he pulled away. The kiss had plagued her for months afterward, but eventually she'd come to the realization that she couldn't erase it any easier than she could erase any other mistake. The problem was she didn't view it as a mistake. And the blow of discovering that he did had been enough to make her hope she'd never see him again.

When, exactly, their relationship had become more, she wasn't sure. Maybe the day he rescued her while stranded out on the lake. Maybe the day he told her Will had died. She and Will had shared a deep love for one another. They knew the other's faults and accepted them willingly. But Savannah couldn't say that Will understood her deep down in her bones the way Logan did.

She still remembered that fateful baseball game all those years ago, the impossibly hot sun above them, and a boy in a Maple Cove High uniform coming up to her. At first she thought he was Logan. It was only after she lifted her hand to shield her eyes from the sun that she realized it was Will, a boy she had always considered a friend. Her eyes had drifted to the dugout for only a second, a part of her searching for Logan even then, but he was nowhere to be found. And besides, they were not the same. Will was her match, a solid guy with a solid family and a solid future.

It had taken her a surprisingly short amount of time to love him, though she would never have said she was *in* love with him. At the time, the idea seemed dramatic and juvenile. Relationships were built on more than silly, overly emotional feelings like love. Still, she respected him and admired him and, for all intents and purposes, loved him. And she would have married him and likely been a very, very happy person.

Because she was blind to the truth.

Her heart belonged to another boy, a boy who had the power to make her fall into a deep, gut-wrenching love, and that boy wasn't Will. The tragedy of it was that she was no longer blind. Her eyes were wide open and her heart so gone it was a wonder she could function without him around. But that man didn't want her, not in a real, tangible way. Not in a work through the tough stuff, fight until you cry, do whatever you must to hold on kind of way. And she wanted that kind of love. She deserved that kind of love.

Sadness took her over as she opened the door to Jim's Hardware, but it held only a second, because the moment she stepped inside, her eyes landed on her sister standing far closer to their handyman than one should unless...

They started to lean into one another and then— Oh my God!

Turning quickly to avoid being seen, Savannah slammed into the person coming in after her, a stand full of postcards toppling over as she jumped back.

"I'm so sorry," Savannah said. She dropped to her knees to pick up the postcards, only to find Patricia Pruitt staring down at her.

Utterly fantastic.

With one glance over her shoulder, she saw that Leigh and Jim were now several feet a part, their cheeks far too red for Savannah to have misunderstood their closeness. Jack was going to kill Jim. Like, chop off his head kill. He'd always been strict with his friends—touch one of his sisters, lose a finger. And though Jack was older now, and dealing with his own problems, she couldn't imagine he'd simply let this go.

Savannah focused on Mrs. Pruitt..

"Oh, good. I was hoping to run into you again."

Savannah set the rack back up and began haphazardly placing the postcards into spots—clearly all the wrong ones, but she couldn't bring herself to ask Jim to direct her.

"Mrs. Pruitt. Nice to see you again." The rack started to fall back over, so Savannah grabbed it, tried to straighten it, and then, realizing she'd likely broken something that made it work, leaned it against the wall. Crap. Jim was going to kill her. She'd have to offer free dinner one night. Or maybe Leigh already gave him free dinner, because they were— She didn't want to think just then about exactly what they were.

Savannah realized in her mental babble she'd missed something Mrs. Pruitt had said. "Sorry, what did you ask?"

"I was hoping you had a free moment to come by the house. I have something for you."

"Oh, um…" She glanced around as if for help, but then her eyes landed squarely on Leigh, who looked like she'd just stolen a hammer and had gotten caught in the act. Gah. Why couldn't she just tell Savannah? Were they really such strangers that she couldn't tell her own sister that she liked Jim?

"I understand if you're too busy."

They were blocking the door now, with several people trying to leave or come in. Having no other choice, Savannah nodded. "Sure. What time?"

"How about now?"

The walk to the Pruitt's home was both absurdly short and impossibly long. Mrs. Pruitt talked about the weather, the upgrades to the elementary school where she taught, anything and everything, as though they were still as close as they once had been. She would have made an amazing mother-in-law, and one of the things that hurt so badly about losing Will was losing his family. His family loved her and she loved them back.

The Pruitts' two-story house sat directly off Rochester Street, one road over from Main. It was one of many on the street, all of them close to the road, sidewalks lining their fronts. Like something out of an old sitcom, it was all smiles and happy times around the kitchen table for breakfast every morning. That was the Pruitt home through and through.

The house was brick, with a white front porch and black shutters, the blinds raised in all the front windows to allow in light. Even after losing their only son, the Pruitt home had a happy vibe to it.

Mrs. Pruitt opened the already unlocked front door and then held it for Savannah.

"Would you like some tea? I know you were always a coffee drinker, but sometimes in the afternoons I like to enjoy tea on the back patio. Would you care to join me today?"

Guilt punched through Savannah's heart at the hopeful expression on her face. She should have come by more often that summer after Will died, asked how she was, made sure she knew Savannah cared. Thankfully, the Pruitts had been away for the last few weeks, so at least her absence now wasn't so noticeable.

"Tea sounds great."

"Earl Grey or English breakfast."

"English breakfast," Savannah answered.

Mrs. Pruitt beamed at her, same as she had the day before at the bed-and-breakfast. "Fantastic. I just need to grab something. Would you mind helping yourself outside? You remember the way?"

"Yes, ma'am."

As she started down the long hall to the deck, memory after memory hit her. Many of them of Will and the smile that never seemed to leave his face, but others were of Logan, tiny details she'd never noticed.

Logan holding open the door for her when they'd eat out back.

Logan switching seats so she could sit beside Will when they watched a movie, his eyes darting to her more than once during the film.

Why hadn't she seen these things before?

Taking her seat outside on the stone patio, the sun bright above, she began to rethink her time around Logan, and each memory brought a new detail, a new encounter with the two of them, until finally there was no denying the truth. She'd thought Logan had hated her when she was with Will, that she was nothing more than the annoying girl who was always around, taking away his best friend. But he was just putting up a front. He'd liked her. Oh God, he'd *liked* her. How could she not have seen it before? All those times after Will died when he talked about always seeing her, the real her, she hadn't realized what he was really trying to say. That whatever happened between them that summer wasn't the start of it for him. It had been going on much longer, the same as it had for her.

"Here we are," Mrs. Pruitt said, slipping out the sliding glass door and setting a tea service down in the center of the table where Savannah sat. Then she handed over a shoebox that she'd rested on the tray. "And this is for you."

Savannah's gaze lingered on the box. "What is it?"

"Some personal things that were Will's. I think he'd have liked you to have them. You can open it now or at home. Either way, I'll understand."

"Oh, no. I can't take this."

Mrs. Pruitt set her hand over Savannah's. "He loved you, dear. So much. He would have wanted you to have this. And he would have wanted you to be happy."

"I am happy."

"Really?" Mrs. Pruitt asked. "Then why does it look like you're about to cry?"

Savannah's gaze traveled to the perfectly landscaped backyard and the white fencing that lined its perimeter. She wondered if Canton Park had been their landscaper, which brought her back to thinking of Logan. "Life's just harder than I thought it would be. They never tell you that, you know?" She focused back on the woman beside her, the woman who had been like a second mother to her when she was a teen. It was weird to view her as a stranger now.

"There is this saying I've always loved. It goes: if the bad times weren't so bad, the good times wouldn't be so good. We need them both to fully appreciate what we have, dear."

"So you're saying…"

Mrs. Pruitt took her hand. "I'm saying, be happy. You have a life, seems a waste not to live it."

They finished their tea, and Savannah said a simple thank you to her dead boyfriend's mother and then set off back home, never in her life gladder to see the road to the bed-and-breakfast.

She'd moved on from losing Logan once, and though she knew it would be hard, she could do it again, but maybe she didn't have to lose him. All during high school, she stayed with Will, never owning her feelings for Logan. Never choosing him. And then that fateful summer when they became so much more and he left, she let him. She didn't call. She didn't try to write. She just allowed him to leave, never fighting for him. Never telling him that she wanted him and no one else.

Well, she did want him. Then and now. And she wasn't willing to let him go so easily this time.

"Thank you for inviting us to breakfast, Logan." Bill poured another cup of coffee from the pitcher Eleanor had placed on their table, dropped in four packets of sugar, then a splash of cream, before lifting the cup to his mouth. How he drank coffee with that much sugar in it was beyond Logan, but he had other worries at the moment.

Alan grunted in agreement, never one to actually say thank you, which suited Logan just fine because he didn't invite them out of the kindness of his heart. He invited them as a last ditch effort. One Hail Mary as the clock wound down. Only Logan feared he was too late. The partners rarely went back on their decisions, and they had their sights set on Maple's B and B. Nothing Logan said would change their minds, but he had to try.

He thought of Savannah's face last night, the sadness he'd put there, and wanted to scream at the partners that this was all their fault. But it wasn't their fault. They were here because Logan had suggested it to them. It was his fault... all of it.

"Everyone should experience Southern Sandwich's French toast," Logan said, his salesman voice turned on. "Best in the South. But actually I wanted to talk to you about the bed-and-breakfast."

Logan sensed ears pricking up from townies seated around him, and he wished he could have found a more private place to sit. He didn't want to have this conversation in Maple, with the whole town in earshot. He wanted to have it back at the office, but the partners had already left the office last night when he called, and fool or not, he wasn't going to call them at home. He was desperate, not suicidal.

"Is there an infrastructure problem? Something major?"

"No, nothing like that." Though Logan wondered if he should have concocted a better reason for this meeting. Some flaw in the bed-and-breakfast that would make it an expensive investment. The problem was that Logan's brain was hardwired to the truth. Good or bad, he never lied. It was likely one of the many results of his upbringing, a positive spin, some might say, though in that moment he could have used a good lie.

"Then what is it?" Alan asked, leaning back in his chair, impatient as always.

This was it, do-or-die time. Logan pulled out the printouts he'd made that morning, noting that he'd have to buy Chloe lunch for a week for sending him the file in the middle of the night. "I no longer feel Maple Cove's Bed and Breakfast is Hartridge and Long's best choice. Stantonville and Harbor Lake each have one as well, both with twice the number of rooms as Maple's for the same price. Plus Harbor Lake would offer the added benefit of boating, both for fishing and scenic pleasure."

Bill looked over the printouts for all of a half minute before glancing back up, his face etched in confusion. "But the real benefit of Maple's bed-and-breakfast has always been the town's charming people." He smiled when Eleanor brought their check, only to find her glaring back. Logan nearly choked on his coffee. That was the thing about Maple—they were charming to each other. Executives here to snatch up one of their prized landmarks? Not so much.

"What is this really about?" Alan asked.

"It's my job to make sure you choose the best investment."

Alan laid down enough cash to cover the check then flipped his gaze back to Logan's. "Yes, it is. And I suggest you remember that. Something tells me your emotional tie to your hometown is clouding your judgment. We have already looked at the properties at Stantonville and Harbor Lake. And the ones in Cherish Pointe and Greenmeadow. Because, while it's your job to ensure we make the best decision, it's our jobs to lay down the capital. We haven't made Hartridge and Long the success it is today by stepping in without knowing all our options."

Logan's jaw tightened at Alan's tone. He wanted to remind the old man that Logan had single-handedly carried the business for the last four years. He'd selected every one of their most profitable investments, not Alan or Bill or any one of the other account executives on staff.

"We appreciate your care in this project, Logan," Bill added, clearly sensing Logan's growing anger, "but we've made our decision. We're buying the Maple property. And now that this breakfast is over, let's head there to take a look."

Logan's stomach turned sour as he led Alan and Bill to the bed-and-breakfast, unsure what else he could do. Refuse to go? Quit? None of that would prevent Alan and Bill from going over, and Logan couldn't let Savannah face them alone. She might hate him forever after this, but he had to go. A part of him prayed that Savannah wouldn't be there, but the other part wanted it to be over. Like ripping off a Band-Aid—smooth and quick. Less pain that way.

But as they walked up the steps, he wondered why he

hadn't warned her? Said something, anything. When he'd returned to his room last night, her door was already closed, the lights out. He pressed his palm to the door, willing her to find some relief from the pain he'd caused her. He supposed he thought he'd be able to convince the partners. Why worry her for nothing? But there was no changing their minds this late in the game, and now...

"Logan. I was wondering where you went," Leigh said, smiling at him. "I was going to ask you to fix—" Her words cut short as she took in Alan and Bill and their business suits. "Who are your friends?" she asked, her voice cautious.

Alan spoke up then. "We're from the firm that is buying this business."

Logan wanted to punch him in the face. How had he worked all these years with such a prick?

"I should get Savannah." She hurried away to the kitchen, and Logan steeled himself for the oncoming nightmare. The nightmare that was his life. He'd been a fool to think he could be happy, and an even bigger idiot to think he could make Savannah happy.

Savannah appeared from the hallway, brushing her hands on her tan cargo skirt to knock off a bit of flour that had found its way there. She smiled at them, which confused Logan, until she spoke.

Stretching out her hand to Alan, she said, "Hi there. My name is Savannah Hale. I understand that you have interest in buying my bed-and-breakfast. Unfortunately, it isn't for sale." Her eyes never drifted to Logan, so he couldn't be sure what went through her mind, but her smile held too long, the corners too tight. Behind the careful facade of a Southern-bred lady lay a raging tiger, seconds from lashing out.

Bill took her hand, then Alan shook it as well before responding. "Ms. Hale, I assure you we will be buying your bed-and-breakfast, whether you give us your blessing or not. We are quite aware of its financial shortcomings. Either you sell it to us and keep a bit of your dignity, or you allow your family's business to go into foreclosure, and we buy it then. It really is no consequence to us at this point, though we would prefer to maintain some grace with the people of Maple Cove."

Logan's hands clenched. Who the hell did Alan think he was? He opened his mouth to tell him as much, job be damned, but a sharp look from Savannah made him hold back. She would handle this herself. She didn't need him.

"Now," Bill said cheerily, trying to put out the fire. Only he didn't know Savannah. There was no calming her down now, no bringing her back to center, no friendly dealings. "We would love to tour the premises. Perhaps have some tea."

"No," Savannah said, her face so red Logan wondered if she would spontaneously combust, like he'd seen on the science channel. "I appreciate you coming here, but the bed-and-breakfast is not for sale. Now, I thank you to please leave."

"Ms. Hale—"

"I said leave!"

Logan came toward her then, torn between maintaining his job and comforting the woman he loved. "Savannah—"

"You lost the right to offer me your opinion when you walked in the door with them. It's time for you to leave." Her gaze met Logan's, hurt and anger fighting it out for control. "All of you."

Jack showed up then, towering over his sisters, his height and build a force to be reckoned with. "You heard her."

Logan cast another glance at Savannah before nodding to the men that they should leave.

"This happens sometimes," Bill said as they walked back down the road, but Logan was no longer listening. He wanted to turn back and say he was sorry, to beg her to forgive him. Beg all three of them to forgive him. But maybe this was for the best. Maybe she could finally move on now.

"Tell me you have good news," Savannah said as she sat down before Frank's desk, eager to hear what her accountant would say. She'd called him the moment Logan had left with his sleazy friends. Though, in truth, they didn't look sleazy, and one of them appeared to be nice enough. Still, they came to take her business, her home, the very bones of her family. How could she be nice? How could she have handled it any differently?

She'd woken this morning to find a note from Logan on the front desk and the words, *Sorry. For everything. x Logan,* scribbled in black ink across the white sheet. Savannah couldn't ignore the irony. His feelings were black and white, with no shades of gray left to interpretation, no hope of something more. She went to his room to find it empty, the bed made, nothing out of place. Like he'd never been there at all. Like he hadn't swept in and stolen her heart, leaving a hole in his wake. How could she talk to him, hear him out, if he'd already left?

Frank settled in his chair, and as his eyes lifted, Savannah knew without him having to say it. "No. Come on, please tell me there's hope." Her bottom lip shook, and this time, she didn't try to stop it. Didn't try to fight away the pain. Memories of her mama poured in. Her kind hugs. Her sweet smile as Daddy sprayed Savannah, Jack, and Leigh with the hose. Her reading to them out on the front porch swing. Making homemade ice cream on the back deck. Listening to stories upon stories from guests by the fire, Savannah and her siblings in awe of the tales.

And now it was all gone. Over. The sign out front forever closed.

"I'm sorry, Savannah. You did your best."

She hung her head. Yeah…and her best wasn't enough.

Chapter Sixteen

A daughter should only ever have to experience the pain of her mother's death once.

But as Savannah reached for another corrugated box, taped up the bottom, and flipped it over to fill with more of her family's things, she felt like her mama had passed all over again. The aching in her chest weighed so heavily she wanted to sit down on the hardwood floor, drop her head into her hands, and cry until she forgot everything. Her mother dying. Losing the bed-and-breakfast. Logan.

Logan.

Pressing her hand to her heart, she rubbed circle after circle, attempting to massage away the pain at his name, but her heart refused to relax. She wondered if it would ever feel contentment again.

"Call him back," Leigh said from beside her.

"There's nothing to say."

They were in the library, packing their daddy's old books,

things he'd picked up during his stints in Scotland, before he finally settled back in Maple and fell madly in love with Jane. Three short months later they were married. That Savannah lost both her parents before they were sixty-five seemed an impossible travesty that she couldn't reconcile. And now the one thing they'd worked their entire lives to preserve was gone. Forget her feelings, she could never forgive Logan for taking the bed-and-breakfast.

He'd called her no less than twenty times, sent text after text, but how could she talk to him now? How could she listen to his voice and not think that he'd taken away the last piece of her parents? Even if she allowed herself to think rationally, to work through the fact that Logan wasn't buying the bed-and-breakfast, his bosses were, it didn't change anything. She would never be able to look at him the same way again.

Leigh dropped another stack of books into a box then looked at Savannah. "There's a lot to say."

"I can't forgive him."

"You don't know that. You haven't heard him out."

Savannah let her gaze drift out the floor-to-ceiling windows of the library, watching as a lazy butterfly flittered around then disappeared out of view into the garden. She thought of her date with Logan out there, how it inspired Romance Under the Stars. How happy the couples had been lying in her garden—how happy she'd been watching them there. "I want to. Forgive him. I mean. I want to so badly it's killing me."

"I know that."

"What would you do if it were Jim?"

Leigh's eyes went wide and she turned away, busying

herself with another shelf. "Why would I care if it were Jim? He's nothing to me."

"It didn't look like nothing at the store the other day."

"He was helping me."

"With what? Cleaning the back of your mouth?"

"Gross."

Just then Jack walked in carrying more boxes, and Leigh pressed a finger to her lips, linked her hands, and mouthed *please*. Savannah nodded, though she didn't like the idea of lying to her brother. She'd have to work that out with her sister later. For now, she had her own problems to worry about.

Her phone buzzed on the coffee table, Logan's name across the screen. Frustration bubbled to the surface. He had no right to call her. Right now, there were only two people in the world who understood what she was going through and they were the only two people she wanted to talk to. Why couldn't he respect that?

"For the love of God, answer the phone or shut the thing off." Jack set the boxes down and began haphazardly tossing things into one.

"I can't. I'm waiting on a call from Frank." She rose up onto her knees to watch Jack toss more of their parents' beloved things into the box, and her frustration turned on him. "Stop it! This stuff is important, and you're going to break something."

Jack spun around, his eyes narrowed. "Name one time you ever saw Dad come in here. He didn't care about this shit; that wasn't how he worked. He cared about people and nothing else. And if you're going to turn that glare on me, I'll call Logan myself and beg him to come over and drag you away."

"Douche," Leigh said, tossing a book at her brother. "You can't call Logan. You can't even talk to him. He's the enemy until Savannah makes her decision."

"Why? I didn't screw him."

Leigh stood now, hands on her hips, and Savannah needed a breather, without her brother and sister's arguing making it impossible to think.

She went out and closed the back door behind her, then walked down the deck's steps, around the two bistro tables she brought in for the patio, and finally into the garden. It was early morning, the sun barely peeking through the leaves, so for once her favorite bench sat empty. A large fountain bubbled a hello as she took her seat and peered around.

Had it really been only three weeks ago that she and Logan were out here? Everything felt so hopeful then— their relationship so new and exiting, the prospect of saving the bed-and-breakfast still a possibility.

She genuinely thought she could save it. In her head, she was already home, Logan beside her, their future so bright it hurt to look at, but she couldn't pull her gaze away. Now, it was all over.

Unable to hold herself up any longer, she lifted her hands to her face and allowed herself to cry for all the hope she'd had and all the things she'd lost. She stayed that way for several minutes, losing herself in her grief, until the snap of a twig snapping made her jerk her head up to find Logan six feet away from her.

"What are you doing here?" she asked as she ran her fingertips under her eyes, trying to hide the worst of the mess. But there was no hiding these tears.

He started for her, and she glared at him. "Don't."

"I—"

"D-don't you dare say you're sorry. Don't you dare, Logan Park." Her voice trembled, and fresh tears sprung into her eyes, but she didn't care. For once she didn't care what anyone thought of her. She was sad. Deep in her muscles and joints, down in the very fibers of her being, she was sad, and she couldn't hide it anymore. A part of her wanted to congratulate him for succeeding in breaking her so completely. She wasn't sure another person could have accomplished the task with such success.

"What do you want from me? What did I…" Her hands shook at her sides, and she drew a breath to try to calm herself down. For years, she wondered who she was more like—her mama or her daddy, but as she stared at the man who'd destroyed her, she knew the answer. Savannah was Jane Hale made over, all heart without sense for where it might lead her. But that didn't mean people should abuse it—and certainly not someone she trusted. "I don't deserve this. Any of it," she said finally, tired and wishing she could take a sleeping pill and forget life for a while.

"No, you don't."

"Then why are you here? To gloat? To tell me that you were right? That my attempts to save my family's home was all a waste? Because *I know*. I know! I still had to try."

"You acted exactly as you should. And there's nothing I can say to fix this, but I am sorry."

She lifted her eyes, rage behind the pain. "For which part? For taking my family's home, or for making me fall in love with you and then leaving me? Again. Because I do love you, and I was ready to fight for you. To tell you that I wanted to try to make this work, that I've loved you for too long not to make this work. But then you packed up all your things without even a good-bye. How could you do that to me?" A sob escaped before she could force it down, and she hunched forward, caving in on herself as the tears won out, and streamed down her face.

Logan reached for her, but she had enough sense and control to toss up a hand, stopping him. A moment passed with nothing but the fountain's melody to fill the air. Finally, Savannah drew a rattled breath and looked up, taking in the man who'd broken her heart now twice. "What do you want, Logan?"

His face reflected all the agony she felt, but she couldn't trust his expression to make her feel better. Nothing could now. "That's why I'm here now. To say good-bye."

If she had any strength at all, she would have laughed. "Of course that's why you're here—you came to say good-bye. Not to try to work on it, to find a way. No, you're just leaving."

"We both knew it would end like this."

Savannah's mouth curved into a sad smile. "See, I thought we were able to choose how it ended. I guess I was wrong there. You'd already decided."

He tucked his hands into his pockets, his eyes glassy as he stared down at her, but he didn't argue. To him, there was no forever, only a ticking clock.

With one more look at him, Savannah bit her trembling lip and breathed out, "Good-bye, Logan," before disappearing back up the walk to what used to be her home.

Logan found himself staring at the Pruitt's house, unsure exactly how he'd ended up there. This wasn't his home, yet while growing up, it was the only place he ever felt relief. And right now, all he wanted was a little relief. He had more regrets than he could bear, each one more complex than the last. How had he let himself get into this mess?

"Logan?"

His eyes rose to see Mrs. Pruitt hanging out the screen door. "Yes, it's me, Mrs. Pruitt."

"I've told you for years to call me Patricia."

He smiled a little. "I'm still working on it, ma'am."

She opened her mouth to say something else, but then closed it as she took him in. "Why don't you come inside? I just made blueberry muffins."

It was long past morning now, and in any other household it might have seemed weird for someone to make muffins after breakfast, but not in the Pruitt home. They never once followed the conventional rules, which was how Logan had ended up staying there as often as he stayed at his own house. Most in Maple turned a blind eye to Canton Park's ways, but not them. It had hurt him tremendously when Will died as much because of their pain as his own. He cared for the Pruitts as family and hated the idea of ever causing them sadness.

He hesitated, and Mrs. Pruitt walked out the door toward him, a white apron around her, with bits of blueberry streaked across it. She stood a good head below him, but as she looked up and pressed a gentle hand to his face, he felt like a small boy again. "Come in, son. Rest your mind."

Logan had to fight back his emotions, but he managed to nod once and follow her into the house. He felt like a traitor for taking their kindness after what he'd done to Will. The thought made him want to apologize for her trouble and walk out, never to bother them again.

Setting down a plate in front of him, along with a tall glass of orange juice, she took the seat beside him and rested her chin in her hand, her eyes full of worry. "Is this about Savannah?"

Logan's head snapped up. "How...?"

She stirred the cup of tea in front of her then rested the spoon on the edge of the saucer. "I'm a mother. We always know. It's okay, you can talk about her here. It feels like whenever I see either of you, you try to pretend the other doesn't exist. But you were both a part of Will's life. And mine. You and Savannah were like my own children. I don't want to see my kids unhappy."

Unsure what to say, Logan took to picking apart his muffin.

"Do you love her?"

His eyes lifted slowly this time. "It doesn't matter if I do. I shouldn't."

"'Shouldn't' isn't a part of love. You either do or you don't, and if you do, and I believe you do, then you shouldn't let the *should* or *shouldn't* stop you from trying to make it work with her. She's a sweet girl. She deserves a good man."

This was the second time someone had said that to him, and he couldn't decide if it made him feel better or worse. "I'm afraid I don't really meet that requirement."

At that she took his hand. "Look at me." He did, because

in Mrs. Pruitt's house you did what she said. "Who fixed the leak in our basement? Who came to visit every day after we lost Will, just to make sure we were okay? You are good, through and through. You've just never seen yourself very clearly. And if you will allow me to say, that's part of the problem with you and Savannah. She's always seen you perfectly clear and I think that scares you."

The throbbing in Logan's head eased a bit as he thought about Savannah, all the things she'd said to him over the years, even before they were…whatever they were. Mrs. Pruitt was right. Savannah knew him and accepted him with nothing but open arms. She offered her heart to him time and time again, only to have him push her away.

He'd messed up, thought about everything the wrong way. He thought because he was Logan Park, only son of the town's trash and Will's best friend, that he wasn't good enough for Savannah. That he didn't deserve her. But that was never his call to make. Savannah loved him, which meant that to her, he was more than simply good enough. He was her match, and she was his, and he was done letting his past control him.

Swallowing hard, he looked at Mrs. Pruitt with a new sense of purpose. Maybe love was never easy. Maybe it was full of anger and sadness and doubts. But if you tried, if you fought for it, love could also be full of joy and happiness and hope. And he had hope that Savannah could forgive him, love him…spend forever with him. "What can I do?"

"I can't answer that. But you can. Women like for our men to fix things. We like to lean on you and to feel like when everything crumbles you can put the pieces back together again. So what does she need you to fix? Figure that out and you have your answer."

Logan stood then, excitement coursing through him, because he knew exactly what she needed him to fix.

"Where are you going?"

He smiled over his shoulder at Mrs. Pruitt as he started for the door. "I'm going to fix it." Hopefully he wasn't too late.

Chapter Seventeen

Savannah took her seat on the plane, her carry-on stashed in an overhead bin, a tote bag in her lap, and her heart full of pain. She still couldn't believe she'd left Maple to return to Boston, and though she knew she'd made the right decision, she ached to change her mind. Ached to beg the pilot to turn around and take her back home. But the B and B was all but gone now. She didn't have a home.

A fresh wave of sadness hit her, and she set the tote on the floor. As she did, she glimpsed a corner of a box from inside. The box Mrs. Pruitt had given her. Savannah had told herself she'd look through it on the plane, but now she wondered if the contents could drive the last nail into her depression coffin.

But then she heard a voice in her head—her mama's as always—telling her to not be afraid. Life went on, fear or not. Might as well go with it.

Lifting the box from her tote, she removed the lid and

peered inside. Will's dog tags rested on top, and as she ran her fingers over them, tears welled in her eyes. Next was an acceptance letter to Duke University. That threw her. He'd never told her he got in. She was surprised he chose the army over Duke, which made her wonder how well she truly knew him.

Below the acceptance was another letter this one folded, but written out—by Will. The words LIFE'S TO-DO LIST ran across the top in Will's writing, and below it was an itemized list of what he wanted to do in his life.

1. Serve in the army.
2. Double major.
3. Work for Hartridge and Long.
4. Explore Europe
5. Backpack through Asia.
6. Safari in Africa.
7. Snowboard
8. Save 5 million dollars
9.

A knot rose in her throat as she stared at the nine, realizing he'd died before he could finish his list. The tears that had threatened her before overflowed now, unable to be contained. He'd only made it through the first thing on his list. Only one thing. She read each of the items again, and then sat up straight, gripping the paper in her hands, a memory coming back to her of a conversation with Logan. *Africa, snowboarding. Backpack through Asia. What do I want to do or what do I need to do?*

Oh my God. She thought maybe Logan had promised

Will that he would do certain things with him. She never realized that Logan was living Will's life, even down to taking the job with Hartridge and Long, a job he seemed to hate, but which he did because Will couldn't. He gave up everything he wanted, even her, all because of his love for his friend.

She closed the box and put it back into her tote, suddenly eager to get off the plane. Eyeing her watch, she sighed. Still ten minutes until she landed in Boston, and then she'd have to try to find a direct flight back to Atlanta, then grab a cab that would take her to Maple. Or maybe she should go directly to his townhome in Atlanta. Only she didn't know where his townhome was and—

"Ugh!"

"Shh," the old man beside her said.

"I'm sorry. I just need to get to Atlanta."

"We just left Atlanta."

"I know that. I need to go back."

The man stared at her like she was crazy, so she shook her head and returned to eyeing her watch, the second hand ticking so slowly and so loudly she was tempted to smash it. Finally, the pilot announced they would be landing, and Savannah sat up tall, eager to get off the plane, so she could— what? Go back? And do what? Tell Logan she knew about the bucket list? Tell him she loved him? She already did that and it wasn't enough. He didn't want her. Still, she had to tell him that she knew about the list, that it was okay to live his life. He was free to be Logan Park now, not some carbon copy of Will.

She turned her phone back on, resolved she would just text him and leave it alone, when her phone buzzed with a new email—a note from Frank.

Dear Savannah,

Please provide me with a fax number to send final paperwork for the deed to your house. I need your signature on a few forms.

Best,
Frank

Savannah stared at the words, sure her brain was intoxicated from all the chocolate she'd eaten on the plane, and could no longer process words properly. Deed to her house? What house? Surely he didn't mean...

Scrolling through her phone, she clicked Leigh's name and grabbed her carry-on from the overhead bin.

"Hey—I need Frank's home number."

"Slow down, what? Are you drunk?"

"No, I need Frank's home number. Can you get it for me?"

Leigh sighed heavily. "Frank doesn't like to be called at home."

"Get me the number."

"Fine. I'll need to make another call, then I'll text it to you."

Savannah's pulse blasted in her ears. None of this made sense. Finally, Leigh texted the number and Savannah stopped just before baggage claim at Logan International to call Frank's house, sure he would be annoyed, but at this point having no choice. She needed to know. Right now.

"Hello?" a groggy voice asked, and Savannah cringed. He sounded half asleep. Crap.

"Um, Frank? It's Savannah Hale. I'm so sorry to bother you at home."

A long pause, then, "I didn't mean you needed to call me with the fax today. Tomorrow would work just fine, so I'll speak with you—"

"Actually, I'm not calling about the fax number. I'm calling about your email. It didn't make sense. A deed? What house? I don't understand."

"The bed-and-breakfast."

Savannah straightened, the phone slipping from her grasp, but she managed to fumble for it before it hit the floor. "What did you say?"

"I said, the bed-and-breakfast. It's yours."

"Mine, but how…?"

She heard him yawn on the other end, then sigh. "The mortgage was paid off by Logan Park. Didn't he tell you? He finalized everything with the bank yesterday. I received the paperwork today. I just need your signature."

"Logan… He… Oh my God."

"I assumed you were going into some dual partnership or what have you. Either way, though, I need your signature to complete the paperwork. Though, not at ten o'clock at night, Ms. Hale."

It took Savannah three seconds to process what this meant, and five more seconds to hang up, grab her carry-on and start toward the exit. Only the moment she looked up, her eyes locked on the very person she'd been so desperate to talk to. He started for her, and tears welled in her eyes.

"What are you doing?" she asked.

Logan swiped away her tear and then cradled her face. "Whatever I have to do. For the rest of my life. I love you and I want to be with you. I want to stand beside you in front of an altar. I want to hold your hand as you give birth to our kids. I want to walk with you on the beach when we're old. I want your forever, and I'm willing to do whatever you want me to do. Because you're my match. You were at ten, and nineteen, and you will be when I'm on my deathbed. I love you."

Unable to remain still another second, Savannah launched into his arms, her lips on his, her heart and mind in sync for the first time. But she had to know if what Frank said was right. Pulling away, she asked, "Is it true?"

"Wha— Oh. It's not a big deal."

"It's everything. It's..." Savannah shook her head, her tears refusing to stop. "You have to let me find a way to repay you. I can pay you monthly, like the bank, something. Anything."

"No. I think I've taken enough from you."

"You've given everything to me...and to Will. I found his list."

At that, Logan straightened, but he didn't say anything.

"I know you've given up your life so he could live his. But I'm here to tell you can stop now. You've fulfilled whatever debt you feel you owe him. You can quit Hartridge and Long if you want, do whatever you like with your life."

"Well, I appreciate that," he said, a hint of a smile in his voice. "But seeing as how they already fired me, I'm not sure they would be interested in a resignation letter."

Savannah sucked in a breath. "No... Logan, I'm so sorry. It's because of the bed-and-breakfast, right? You have to let me call them. I can tell them I forced you into it. Blackmail or something. I can come up with a lie that you—"

"Stop talking," he said, one hand gliding into her hair as the other tilted her chin up, "and kiss me." His lips met hers, and in them lay all the hurt and pain, the longing and hope. He pulled away then to look at her. "I'm sorry I left eight years ago. But you have to know, you have to see that it was all for you. It was my way of loving you. Because I do—love you. I love you to the depths of my soul, and I may never deserve you, but if you'll let me, I'll spend the rest of my life trying to."

"I understand now, and while I will always love Will for the wonderful person he was, he never had my heart. You did. You do."

A smile broke across Logan's face. "Are you trying to tell me that you love me?"

"I'm trying to tell you that I *always* loved you. And I *will* always love you."

Epilogue

One year later

Savannah stood just inside the basement door, forcing herself not to peek outside, butterflies swarming in her stomach.

"Are you ready?" Jack asked, and she turned to see him dressed in the dark gray suit they'd chosen for him, a matching tie, a smile on his face and no hint of the humor he typically wore around his older sister. "You look beautiful."

Savannah's gaze dropped to her dress— strapless, white satin with silver and gold stitching, beading in all the right places. It was the most beautiful thing she'd ever seen.

Taking her arm, Jack opened the door and Savannah drew a short breath at the sight of the garden, flowers everywhere, the smell of honeysuckle in the air, the string quartet playing "Canon in D" at its center. And then she stopped at the end of the white cloth aisle, now covered in white and pink rose petals, and her eyes locked on the man at the other end. On her soon to be husband.

On Logan.

A boom of thunder hit overhead, followed by a crack of lightning, causing the crowd to gasp, but still Logan's eyes held steady on her. The song switched to The Civil Wars' "Poison & Wine"—their song—and she started toward Logan. Tiny droplets of water dripped from the sky like a faucet left on. Still, she kept her pace.

Jack stopped them before Pastor Parkins and Logan, his hand still covering Savannah's. "Promise to be good to her," he said to Logan, who nodded once.

"You have my word."

Jack passed Savannah's hand to Logan, and their eyes locked just as the dark sky opened up, showers drenching the garden and everything in it, but neither Savannah nor Logan moved.

"Should I continue?" Pastor Parkins asked, as another bolt of lightning hit.

The rest of the crowd ducked back into the safety of the bed-and-breakfast, except Leigh, the maid of honor, and Jim, the best man.

"Mama always said rain on a wedding day was good luck."

Logan smiled. "I can't wait another minute to call this woman my wife."

Savannah's heart surged, and she leaned in—just as Pastor Parkins cleared his throat. "We aren't to that part yet, Ms. Hale."

She grinned. "Right."

"Dearly beloved, we are gathered here to witness the union of Savannah Hale and Logan Park…"

But Savannah lost track of the words as she stared into

her love's eyes, the words "I do" coming out of his mouth, and then hers, and then, "You may kiss the bride," had only a moment to register before Logan pulled her to him, his lips crushing down on hers. Time seemed to stop as they kissed, their cup of happiness running over.

At some point Pastor Parkins stepped around them and went inside, followed eventually by Leigh and Jim. Yet still they continued to kiss, allowing the warmth of their love to spread through them, refusing to let go.

Forever.

Acknowledgments

There are so many people to thank for this book that I'm super scared I will forget someone.

First, as always, thank you God, for your strength and guidance and ability to humble me when I need it the most.

For my superstar agent, Nicole Resciniti—I'm not sure I could produce a book now without sending you a thousand emails with plot ideas/character ideas/general craziness. Thank you for being such a wonderful person to lead me through this business.

Thank you to my amazing editor, Alycia Tornetta. Working on a book with you is so painless and natural. Every step has been a true joy as I learn from your insight. Thank you! And a huge thank you to Crystal Havens for being so thorough and always a joy to work with, and to the rest of the editorial and publicity teams with Entangled Publishing, thank you!

This book would not exist without the guidance of

several men and women in the military and several military wives. I have so much respect for what you do--those who fight and those who hold down the fort at home. You are all heroes in my book. A special thanks to Erika Douglas, Laura Boggs, and Sarah Ramos for answering direct questions and allowing me to ask questions that by all accounts shouldn't be asked. Your help is the reason this book has the depth it needs. Thank you.

A giant, huge, loud thanks to Cindi Madsen and Rachel Harris for all the texting and emails and support over not only this book, but all my books. I feel so blessed to call you friends!

Thank you to my husband Jason, who is the reason I can write romance at all. Thank you for being such an amazing man and father. I love you more every day. And thank you to my lovely daughters, who keep me laughing and sane. You are my heart. And thank you to the rest of my family and friends, who support me continuously and help me through the highs and lows of this business. I adore each of you.

Finally, a big thanks to you, my readers. Thanks to members of Mel's Madhouse and all my readers. Thank you for taking the time out of your day to live in my characters' world. Thank you for talking about my books to your friends, for posting reviews, for being so wonderful. I truly couldn't write without you!

About the Author

Melissa West writes heartfelt Southern romance and teen sci-fi romance, all with lots of kissing. Because who doesn't like kissing? She lives outside of Atlanta, Georgia, with her husband and two daughters, and spends most of her time writing, reading, or fueling her coffee addiction.

Connect with Melissa at www.melissawestauthor.com or join her reader group https://www.facebook.com/groups/MelsMadhouse/.

New Adult books by Melissa West...

NO KISSING ALLOWED

Young adult books by Melissa West...

GRAVITY

HOVER

COLLIDE

www.ingramcontent.com/pod-product-compliance
Lightning Source LLC
Chambersburg PA
CBHW030313200626
46816CB00002BA/879